Always Devoted

Always Devoted

Search for Love Series

KAREN ROSE SMITH

ABOUT THE AUTHOR
Karen Rose Smith

Award-winning author Karen Rose Smith was born in Pennsylvania. Although she was an only child, she remembers the bonds of an extended family. Since her father came from a family of ten and her mother, a family of seven, there were always aunts, uncles and cousins visiting on weekends. Family is a strong theme in her books and she suspects her childhood memories are the reason.

In college, Karen began writing poetry and also met her husband to be. They both began married life as teachers, but when their son was born, Karen decided to try her hand at a home-decorating business. She returned to teaching for a while but changes in her life led her to writing romance fiction. Now she writes romances and mysteries full time. She has sold over 80 novels since 1991.

Presently, she is hard at work on a series for Harlequin Special Edition as well as the Caprice De Luca home stager mystery series for Kensington Books. When she isn't writing, she cares for three rescue cats, gardens, and cooks. Married to her college sweetheart since 1971, believing in the power of love and commitment, she envisions herself writing relationship novels, both romance and mystery, for a long time to come!

Always Devoted

Chapter One

"What do you believe happened to your sister?"

Emma Henderson felt her throat tighten and she found swallowing difficult. She hated the glare of the television lights and found her gaze swinging away from the camera to offstage where Linc Granger stood. The successful TV producer, who garnered high ratings with his specials, had convinced her this interview might help find Paige. That was the only reason she'd agreed to do it.

"I don't know what happened to Paige, Ms. Kahill. She left one afternoon to drive to San Francisco for the weekend and I haven't seen her since." Emma's voice cracked.

She almost felt Linc Granger take a step forward. To do what? Stop the interview with journalist, Tessa Kahill? To comfort her? To tell her everything was going to be okay when she knew it wasn't?

"Her car was found on the shoulder of the highway and she was missing. Can you tell me what your thoughts were when you found out?" the world-renown journalist asked.

"I was stunned. I couldn't believe it. At first we all thought she might have been kidnapped. But there was no call...no note for ransom...nothing."

"You were on the police list of persons of interest for a while, weren't you?"

"Tessa!" Linc Granger's deep voice rent the air with authority. He told the technicians to cut and take five. Then he strode up beside the interviewer.

His gaze connected to Emma's for a heart-stopping moment.

She tore her eyes from his and took a deep breath. She shouldn't have this reaction to him. He'd been compassionate toward her, protective even, and she was grateful. That's all there was to it.

But as Linc and the beautiful, curly-haired interviewer argued over the questions for the remainder of the interview to be aired later in the week, Emma knew she felt a spark of something with Linc Granger she'd never felt with her late husband Barrett.

After another minute or two of discussion, Linc crossed over to her chair and towered over her. He raked his hand through his dark brown hair, his green eyes turbulent. "Tessa insists she has to go this route. She thinks it's better if everything is out there in the public's face. I don't necessarily agree. I know you lost your husband a year ago and this is hard. If you'd rather Tessa go in a different direction—"

As Emma shook her head, her honey-blond hair fell over her shoulder. "The family is always questioned. The family is always of interest. It's okay, Mr. Granger."

"It's Linc," he said gently. As cutting as his voice had been a few moments before, it was so different now.

Ever since their first meeting, she'd felt strangely out of breath. She was a mother with a four-year-old, and her sister was missing. She couldn't think about anything else.

Squaring her shoulders, she assured him, "I can handle Ms. Kahill's questions."

As Linc Granger studied her, she felt almost all of the air get sucked out of the room. What was it about him that made her so flustered? He was older, between thirty-five and forty she guessed, and she felt young at twenty-six for the first time in years. She'd taken on a lot of responsibility early.

After a few moments, he reassured her again. "If anything makes you too uncomfortable, you can say so. I'm sorry I wasn't here when the interview started. I would have laid down some ground rules." He glared at Tessa as she was studying her notes.

"When you offered me the opportunity to publicize Paige's disappearance again, you said Tessa Kahill was the best. Maybe you should let her do her job. Before we started, she told me she has to be on a plane out of L.A. tonight to Afghanistan."

"You like her," Linc noted with a wry smile.

"We talked before the interview. Yes, I do. And I respect her."

"Good." He sounded relieved. "Then I'll let her continue and I won't interfere again. But I would like to discuss something with you when this is over. Do you have time?"

What could he want to discuss with her? They'd spoken at length about what had happened to Paige, the little bit she knew, and Emma's desire to stay out of the spotlight for her daughter's sake. But he seemed to have something important to say and she did want to hear it.

"My next door neighbor is watching Becky. I'll have some time."

He was quiet for a few moments, but the intensity of his expression suddenly gave her the knowledge that Linc Granger was a very different man than Barrett Henderson had been.

It shouldn't matter.

But she found herself wanting to listen to Linc, even though she suspected that simple conversation with him could unsettle her life even more.

What a stupid thing to do!

Linc never interrupted the flow of an interview. When he'd asked Tessa to do this, she'd told him she could fit it in during a layover in L.A. She'd been in Mexico interviewing some diplomat, and then she was gone again for Afghanistan to tape a special report.

So why had he jumped in?

Because Emma Trent Henderson fascinated him. She and her four-year-old daughter had been through the cable newsringer when her sister had disappeared three months ago. Yet she'd somehow retained her dignity and poise. Still, the lost look in her expressive brown eyes when she spoke about her sister, Paige, haunted him.

From her first press conference, he'd been intrigued by her and her story. Maybe because he knew someone who could help her if she wanted to be helped. Unorthodox means weren't for everyone, but he had the feeling Emma had exhausted the usual channels.

The cameras were rolling again and Tessa was asking more questions. As he listened to the rest of the interview, he became more sure about the information he wanted to give Emma. When he heard Tessa end her questions with, "Tell me how you feel as a widow, with a four-year-old to raise and no idea where your sister is," he listened hard.

Emma didn't hesitate to say softly, "Sometimes I feel as if I'm in limbo. I'm searching for answers and I don't know if I'll ever find them."

Linc knew he had to tell Emma about Gillian Bradley and her special gift.

When Emma finished the interview, she felt wrung out. Not a new feeling these days. But after she thanked Tessa, she turned to find Linc waiting for her. It was easy for her to think of using his first name and she wasn't sure exactly why.

She'd worn a flowered sundress for the interview, a dress she often wore when taking sales orders in her gift basket shop, *Occasional Baskets*. But now she wished she'd worn something a little more sophisticated...because Linc Granger in his custom-tailored suit, tie and expensive shirt shouted sophistication.

Who was she kidding?

She'd never been sophisticated. Hard working and tasteful, maybe, but never sophisticated.

After the camera lights shut down and she stood, Linc took her elbow. She felt the heat from his fingers through her whole body. It was an odd, wake-up feeling that she'd never experienced with Barrett.

Barrett. He'd only been gone a year. How could she even be attracted to someone else?

Okay, so that's what this feeling was toward Linc Granger...attraction. So much for that. He certainly didn't drive his car in her neighborhood.

Linc glanced around the set where techs were bustling by and men in suits strode purposefully here and there. He frowned.

Even frowning, his face was ruggedly handsome with character lines around his eyes that cut deep. From laughter? Or worry?

Turning his focus back to her, he asked, "My car service picked you up, right?"

"Yes, thank you. It was nice to relax for a change driving into the city."

He smiled, and then the smile slipped away. He actually looked uncertain for a moment, but only for a very fleeting moment. "We're not going to find privacy here," he explained. "Even in my office I'm constantly interrupted. Would you consider taking a drive? I have a place on the beach—"

At her surprised expression he held up his hand in a "stop" gesture. "This is not a proposition," he assured her, his voice lowering. "I can even provide you numbers of a few good friends if you want to check me out. I just believe we need privacy for this discussion."

And just what discussion was it? "I checked you out before I agreed to do this interview," she admitted. "At least as much as I could."

He looked mildly amused. "So, what did you find when you checked me out?"

"I found out that everything you do pretty much turns to gold. You went to Cal State for a degree in Cinema and TV Arts. You directed a couple of small films, afterward turning that money over into investments. Then you started gathering professionals around you who wanted to make the same films and then TV shows that you did. You've produced cable documentaries as well as network hits. But that all involves business, not your character or your personal life."

"My personal life is off limits to reporters." That was said without any amusement at all.

"I did find a couple of Google images with you escorting celebrities or models to charity functions and social galas. But that really didn't tell me much."

His eyebrows arched, thick eyebrows over deep green eyes that made her feel a little fluttery inside. Okay, maybe a lot fluttery inside.

"So why did you decide to do the interview?" he asked.

"Because I found transcripts of other interviews you produced. They were honest and considerate of whomever was being interviewed. I also liked your..." She hesitated. "Your point of view when we talked. I didn't feel you were going to sensationalize what had happened to me. You proved it just now when you stepped in."

The nerve in his almost-square jaw worked for a moment. Then that small giveaway of tension was gone. "I want to discuss something other than letting the police direct the investigation to find your sister."

That's all she needed to hear. "Let's go for that drive."

A half-hour later they were in Linc's sporty silver luxury sedan, heading toward the ocean. Up until now they'd made small talk about the interview, about Tessa, about Emma's daughter who was learning so fast and growing so much. She'd called Becky's sitter before they'd left to make sure Maris and her daughter could find something for supper if she wasn't back in time.

At a lull in the conversation, Emma watched Linc's large hands on the steering wheel. He'd discarded his suit jacket and tie and opened the top two buttons on his shirt before he'd climbed into the car. Sitting beside him like this, the atmosphere seemed oddly intimate as the day started winding down and the sun sank lower on the horizon.

"Not much longer," he told her.

She sent him a small smile. "Am I looking impatient?"

"No, just a little nervous. Are you sure you don't want to call my best friend?"

That probably would have been wise. But Linc seemed straightforward. "Tell me about your best friend."

After Linc cut her a glance, he focused on the highway again. "His name is Nathan Bradley. He's a family man with two daughters from his first marriage he sees a lot, and a little boy, Matthew, from his second marriage. He's an internet security expert who flies all over the country, taking care of important people's networks."

"I like the fact that you put his family history before his work."

"Would it make you feel better if I told you I babysit for Nathan? I did before he married Gillian and I do now. Their kids call me Uncle Linc."

She laughed. "Maybe I should talk to *them*."

He laughed, too, and glanced at her again. Something intangible passed between them that she seemed to feel in her heart. How crazy was that?

Fifteen minutes later, Linc turned off the highway and took a series of turns. After he drove down a long drive, they exited the car and Emma looked around.

A one-story house sprawled before her and she could see the ocean beyond. "What a beautiful setting," she murmured.

"I like it. It's worth the commute. We're alone here. If you prefer to walk the beach instead of going inside, I'll understand."

Alone with Linc Granger. Maybe she should have trepidations about that, but she didn't. She felt excited. Because they were going to talk about a way to find her sister? Or because he was one very sexy man?

Because he was going to give her information to find a way to find Paige, of course.

"I'll shed my shoes and we can walk the beach," she decided, taking the safer route.

"Give me five minutes to get comfortable and then we'll walk. There's a deck around back. Would you like something to drink?"

"No, I'm fine."

"Be right back."

Emma found cushy chairs and chaises on his deck,

but she was too fidgety to sit. Instead, she stood at the railing, looking out at the ocean, wondering if her sister was still alive and if she was, *where* she was. She'd spent so many hours while Paige had been gone thinking about that—praying, hoping and trying to stay positive. But how could she when such dark visions invaded the others? Paige's car wasn't worth the bald tires it had been running on, so no one would have wanted to hijack her car. Had she had engine trouble again, left the vehicle and started walking? Had someone picked her up and then—

There were those dark thoughts that Emma didn't want to have, but knew she had to be realistic about.

When Linc emerged from the house he wore a blue polo shirt and denim cutoffs. His feet were bare.

"Ready?" he asked.

"Ready to find my sister," she agreed.

She kept her shoes on until they reached the bottom of the wooden steps where grass and sand began. Then she took them off and laid them on the step. Sea grass tickled her legs as they made their way across the sand to the packed beach.

As they walked along the shore, the wind tossing their hair, Linc asked, "Do you believe in things you can't see?"

Her gaze met his. "You mean religion?"

He blew out a breath. "No, that's not what I mean. I'm just going to lay this all out," he said. "If you want to walk back to my house, get in the car and go home, that's fine. But I felt this was an option you should consider."

"You're not talking about a private investigator, are you?" The spray from the ocean misted them as they left their footprints on the shoreline.

"Sort of."

"Linc, I can't afford one. I hired someone the first week after Paige disappeared. But he couldn't find anything and I couldn't afford to have him go on looking. When Barrett died, he didn't have life insurance. It was one of those things he kept putting off doing. Thank goodness I had my business, but with insurance costs and the mortgage, I don't have much left over each month."

Linc stopped and took her arm. Again his touch made her tummy somersault and her pulse race. But she had to focus on what they were discussing, not her reactions to him.

"Emma, this isn't about money. It's about a gift my best friend's wife has. Nathan's wife, Gillian, works with another friend of mine, Jake Donovan. Jake used to be a cop. Then he turned to private investigation. But after he met Gillian, his life changed. For the most part he and Gillian find missing persons, especially lost children. They started a foundation for this purpose. People they've helped have donated a lot of money. Funds just seem to stream in because it's a good cause."

"So Nathan's wife, Gillian, is a private investigator, too?"

"No, she's not. Nathan found Gillian through Jake as a last-ditch effort when his ex-wife disappeared with his daughters. Gillian found them for him. She has a gift. Some people would label her a psychic. She doesn't think of herself that way. She just seems to be able to tune in to missing persons. She gets sensations and feelings and in themselves they're not enough. But when family members are questioned, or Jake does research tracking down information Gillian gets, they've got a 99% success rate."

Emma was astonished by what Linc was telling her. He was a rational businessman and yet he obviously believed in what he called Gillian's gift.

"Let's walk some more," she said to Linc, pulling her arm from his clasp because she couldn't think straight with his hand on her skin.

Silent as they walked, he glanced at her every now and then. She could feel that glance, feel his concern and compassion for her.

Finally she said, "My dad left after Paige was born.

We never heard from him again. My mom was really hurt by his abandonment. When she felt hurt, she went to church, taking us with her for the same comfort she found there until she died of breast cancer."

Linc stopped walking again. "I'm sorry."

She could see he wasn't just saying the words, he was sorry. And there was a deeper understanding in his expression that made her wonder about his background. "Thank you. The reason I'm telling you this is—before mom died, she took my hand and she made me promise that I would take care of Paige and if I ever had children that I would take them to church. She thought everyone needed to believe in something outside of themselves, just like she did and just like Paige and I did."

"Do you take Becky to church?"

"I do most weeks. She attends Sunday School while I go to the service. So what I'm trying to say is that I believe in something outside of myself." She looked toward the ocean and waved her hand. "I believe in the power behind this."

Facing him again, she requested, "So tell me more about Gillian."

"The way I understand it, when she was ten she was hit by lightning. It was after that the sensations started to come to her. She's a caring person. She loves her husband and son, and Nathan's daughters accept her as a second mom."

"And she teamed up with a former cop."

"Jake had heard about her, looked into her success rate and then recommended her to Nathan. After she found Nathan's daughters, Jake was a believer."

"Are you sure there's no fee, Linc? I can make a donation, but I don't know how much."

"They don't charge."

"But you've donated to this foundation," she guessed.

"I have. I believe in the work they do."

Emma stared at the sun beginning to set, the sky shot through with pink and orange. She thought about Paige and the empty car and dark nights when she couldn't sleep wondering where her sister was, crying because she was afraid Paige had been hurt, crying because she was afraid she was dead.

"Let's walk back," she said, needing to think about all of this.

Linc didn't initiate conversation as they walked, as gulls screeched, as waves pounded the shore. The tide was coming in, creating puddles in the sand that she was barely aware of as she sloshed through them. Linc stayed by her side, walked where she walked, a force to be reckoned with himself.

She would have kept walking, but Linc tapped her shoulder and pointed to his house across the expanse of loose sand and grass. When they reached the steps, she wiped the sand from her feet and slipped them into her shoes. He let her precede him.

Once they were standing on the deck, she made a decision. The ocean wasn't as loud up here but it still carried a resonant voice, a pounding that was a backdrop.

When she turned to face Linc, for a few moments the sound of the ocean faded away. The brush of the breeze on her face hardly registered because she got lost in his green eyes. But then she remembered why she was here, at his house on the beach.

Her voice was loud and clear above the sound of the surf. "I'd like to meet Gillian."

Chapter Two

When Linc pulled up in front of Emma's bunga-low, pretty much the same as every bungalow on the street except for the orange poppies and Red-buds around the foundation, the pretty wreath on the door, he was feeling disconcerted to say the least. He didn't like his attraction to Emma Henderson.

Plain and simple, he didn't trust most women. His parents' divorce had been brutal. His mother had only wanted custody of him to win the war. She made up garbage about his dad, how he lost his temper, how he was never home, how he went to the bar with his bud-dies to drink. But Linc knew his dad only lost his tem-per when his mother ran up their credit card bill or when she forgot about Linc's track meet or when she had too many drinks at a party they attended. And as far as working late? He'd had to pay for their debt. A drink with his buddies at a nearby sports bar on Friday afternoons was as far as that went.

Linc had been old enough to know the truth. By twelve he'd learned to distrust his mother's motives about everything. She'd wanted a huge divorce settlement and she'd gotten it.

Emma hadn't been able to find personal information on him because he was careful not to put it out there. And if it got out, Nathan's internet skills managed to block it or make it disappear.

Once he'd thought he'd risk getting married. Colleen had seemed not to care about his money or his name or his success. But he'd been bamboozled by her and had learned the truth the hard way. She'd had an abortion and hadn't told him. He'd found out by accident when she'd been in another room and he'd picked up her cell phone, thinking he was doing her a favor. He'd answered a call from a clinic confirming a follow-up appointment. When he'd looked into that clinic and then confronted Colleen, he'd learned the truth. She didn't want children. She wasn't about to lose her figure to a baby or be chained down caring for one.

How had he been so blind? Maybe he'd just wanted a family too badly.

He loved spending time with Nathan and Gillian,

enjoying their kids, and with Jake and Sara and their little boy. Over the past few months he'd been seriously considering adopting kids of his own. Why not? There were plenty of kids out there who needed a home.

As Linc stared at the front door of the bungalow, he somehow knew in his gut that this was a home.

Linc hadn't been able to reach Gillian on her cell. Sometimes she went hiking with Nathan where there wasn't any cell phone reception. Sometimes she and Jake had to make a trip to search for missing persons. If she was flying, her cell would be turned off.

"Why don't you come in for a cup of coffee? Then we can try Gillian again," Emma said. "I'd really like to set up an appointment as soon as we can. If I can't be in my shop, I have to juggle my salesclerks."

Should he go into Emma's house for a cup of coffee? There was a car in the carport and he assumed that was hers. "Is your daughter at your neighbor's?"

"No. Maris watches her here. If we didn't do it that way, Becky would want to take everything but the kitchen sink over there."

Linc shook his head. "Kids and their toys. I bought Nathan's little boy, Matthew, a monster truck for Christmas. All he wanted to do was play with the box."

Emma's smile as she thought about children and maybe her daughter was devoid of the confusion and turmoil that had been there when she'd talked about her sister. "Becky's into crafts right now. She likes pasting cotton balls on a piece of paper to make a lamb or pasting popcorn kernels on a drawing to decorate a tree."

"An artist in the making," Linc suggested.

"Maybe. But I think she just likes the mess it makes."

Linc laughed. He enjoyed Emma's down-to-earth way of looking at life. A cup of coffee with a four-year-old chaperone didn't seem like a bad idea. But as Linc followed Emma to the side door, he watched the natural sway of her hips in her heels. He also glimpsed her long, creamy neck as she pushed her hair over her shoulder. When he again caught the scent of the flowery perfume she was wearing, his body told him coffee, even with a chaperone, could be an ordeal.

She wasn't asking him inside for a rendezvous, he told himself. She was asking him inside because she wanted to find her sister.

Linc had guessed this door would lead into a kitchen and he was right. He stepped inside behind Emma, into a charming blue-and-yellow flowered country charm ambience.

As soon as the little girl sitting at the kitchen table saw Emma, she scrambled off her chair and came running toward her. "Mommy. Mommy. You're home!"

Emma stooped and hugged her daughter, gathering

her close. "I've missed you, honey," Emma said, hugging her, tickling her and blowing a kiss in her ear.

Her daughter giggled. "I'm making cereal houses."

"Cereal houses?" Emma stood and her gaze met an older woman's. Her baby sitter was sitting at the table with a crayon in her hand. "We've been making a whole village."

Emma released her daughter and stood and introduced Linc. "Maris Stambaugh, this is Linc Granger. He produced the interview I told you about. It will air in a few days."

Maris came forward and shook his hand. "It's good to meet you. I hope the interview helps bring Paige home."

"I do, too. We'll be doing plenty of promo for it, including on the social networks."

Emma's arm was around her daughter's shoulders. "Becky, I'd like you to meet a new friend of mine. This is Mr. Granger."

He crouched down to Becky's eye level. "You can call me Linc."

Becky ducked behind her mom's sundress skirt and peeked out at him, only her little face—a very much younger version of Emma's—visible.

"She's often shy around new people," Emma explained.

"That's understandable," Linc said, still crouched down. "Becky, can you call me Linc?"

She screwed up her little face. "Linc?"

He laughed. "Success! How many houses do you have in your village?"

She seemed torn between her shyness and wanting to tell him. He waited, knowing that's what you had to do with kids.

Finally, Becky looked up at her mom. Emma nodded, as if it was okay to reveal such important information to him.

Suddenly Becky's arm appeared from behind her mom's skirt and she held up two fingers. But then she added, "We're makin' more."

"Maybe you can paint a few of those cereal pieces silver and make a car, too."

"Don't give her any ideas," Emma chided. "Have you been around paint and four-year-olds?"

He chuckled. "I usually don't have to handle the cleanup." Then he addressed Becky again. "Do you want to show me your pictures?"

This time she forgot about being shy. She ran over to the table, grabbed one and brought it to him. "It's dry!" she proclaimed proudly.

"Good thing, too," Emma said wryly, noting the pieces of circular cereal all over the table and a few scattered on the floor.

Linc gave the picture the proper attention it deserved,

then he rose to his feet. "Would you like to show me the ones that aren't dry?"

Nodding vigorously, Becky led him over to the table.

He caught Emma studying him curiously. Then she was in motion. "I'll make that coffee."

As the coffee pot gurgled and spit, Emma watched Linc with her daughter. He really *did* seem to like kids. His talk about spending time with his friends' children must have been the truth.

Why wouldn't she expect the truth? Because Barrett had lied to her on occasion—nothing big, just a little white lie here and there. He'd tell her he was working late. He was an accountant with his own office. But then she'd find out he was really playing poker with friends. Why he hadn't just told her that in the first place, she could never figure out. He'd tell her he'd be home for supper at 5:00, but not actually come home until around 7:00. It was as if he wanted to keep her off balance. Maybe it had just been a control issue.

After Maris left, Emma noted that Linc was still talking to her daughter, helping her arrange cereal on another house. Every once in a while they'd each snitch a piece and eat it. Barrett hadn't played with Becky, hadn't cooed to her, rocked her, or fed her. That had been Emma's responsibility, and she'd loved doing it. But she'd felt so alone, like the things that really mattered to her hadn't mattered to Barrett. Having a little girl to raise was something he put up with and didn't enjoy. When they were dating and first married, he'd been charming and considerate. But after Becky was born, their marriage had changed. *He* had changed and she hadn't known what to do about it.

Becky's voice suddenly pierced her musings. "Can Linc read a book with us?"

"Oh, I don't know, honey. Linc's a busy man. He might not have time."

Linc looked down at her daughter and then up at her. When their gazes met, she felt the room shake a little. It was an entirely disturbing feeling and one she wasn't used to. She tried not to let *anyone* rock her world, but this man was succeeding in more ways than one.

He said, "I have to make a phone call. But I do have time. It's up to your mom, though. Reading a book before bed is pretty special. You don't just share that with anyone."

He was telling her it was okay if she didn't want him farther into her house, okay if she didn't want him to move farther into her life. Confused by her attraction to him, but recognizing the way he was making her daughter feel special, she agreed to Becky's request. "Okay, honey. Do you think you can get cleaned up there?"

"Can you help?" she asked Linc, who definitely seemed to be her new friend.

"I can if your mom has a dustpan. Somehow the cereal seemed to jump all over the floor."

Becky giggled.

Emma knew the cleanup wouldn't take long. But when she took the dustpan off the hook in the closet and handed it to Linc, they seemed to be standing very close together. He took up all the space in her kitchen. He was so tall, so broad-shouldered, so slim-hipped, so…sexy. Her mind went places it hadn't been for a very long time.

As he took the dustpan from her, he gave her a crooked smile, as if he seemed to know what she was thinking. She felt flustered all over again. She wished he could reach Gillian Bradley and reach her quickly.

Linc took out his phone while she readied Becky for bed. She was picking out a book from the shelf when he entered the purple-and-yellow flouncy bedroom. It was pure little girl with its white dresser, bookshelves, desk and single bed, its lilac curtains and purple comforter. Becky's favorite color was purple, so Emma had given in to her daughter's desire to have the color everywhere. But Linc seemed like a giant in the room and Emma realized it wasn't just his tall, fit build—it was his presence. He emanated confidence and power.

He answered her question without her having to ask. "Still not answering. Nathan isn't either, which makes me think—" He gave a shrug. "They don't have many evenings alone, so they might be taking advantage of this one."

Emma knew she and Barrett hadn't done that often enough. Maybe if they had, they would have grown together in their marriage instead of apart.

Linc reassured her, "I've left messages. Gillian will get back to me as soon as she can."

In the same small room, Emma couldn't ignore the electricity that was zipping back and forth between her and Linc. Totally impossible, she told herself again. Impossible.

But when Linc hunkered down beside Becky and asked, "Which are your favorite books?" and helped her pick out one they both liked, Emma sighed with an almost resigned acceptance of what she was feeling. She wanted to touch his broad back. She wanted to run her fingers through his thick brown hair. She wanted to—

Nope, she didn't. Not here, not now. Not anywhere, not anytime. Since Becky's bed was a single, Linc sat on one side of her daughter on the side of the bed and Emma sat on the other.

"Can *you* read?" Becky asked Linc.

Surprised, Emma glanced at him. He seemed unfazed by her daughter's request. "Sure." He pointed up at the ceiling where silver stars were painted in a variety of constellations. "What are those?"

Becky giggled. "My stars. We count them before I go to sleep."

"What a great idea," Linc said, glancing over at Emma as if she were a very smart mom. His admiration felt good.

Even with Becky between them, Emma was aware of his bare hair-roughened legs in the cutoffs, his muscled forearms as he held Becky's book, the deep timbre of his voice as he read. He seemed so comfortable, she wondered how many times he'd read to his friends' children.

After the story was finished, Becky looked up at Linc as if she expected something from him. How easily she could get attached. She saw her friends' daddies pushing them on swings, helping them on jungle gyms. She knew her daddy had gone away somewhere and was never coming back. Like Emma herself when she was a child, did Becky long for a father who would give her hugs and kisses and was always there when she needed him?

Linc didn't seem to want to overextend any boundaries. He flipped up the end of one of Becky's pigtails.

"It was nice meeting you, Becky. Thanks for inviting me to read one of your books." He stood. "You have lots of sweet dreams."

Then he walked out of her daughter's bedroom briskly, saying over his shoulder to Emma, "I'll make that call again." His words seemed a bit terse and Emma wondered what had happened.

After she tucked Becky in, counted stars, kissed her goodnight and turned on the night light, she closed her daughter's door part way and went to the living room. The house she and Barrett had bought had fit their income level. Barrett had always told her it was just temporary, until they could afford something bigger. But Emma had always been happy here. Her living room was comfortable, decorated in tan, russet and navy. Some of Becky's dolls lay scattered across the sofa, plastic animals littered the coffee table.

Linc was standing by the picture window talking on his phone, staring out into the dark night. He ended his call as she crossed to him, hopeful now that he'd reached Gillian Bradley.

"Gillian and Nathan had gone to dinner. They'd switched off their phone for a while. She'd been about to call me. She said she'd be glad to meet with you, but that you shouldn't expect too much. She never knows what will happen."

"When?" Emma asked, thinking only of her sister now. For a short time tonight, she'd been able to set aside stress and worry, probably because her attraction to Linc had given her something else to think about.

"If we meet with her tomorrow morning, she said Nathan can watch Matthew. Does that work for you?"

"Becky has preschool tomorrow. I drive her there around 8:30. It's a few blocks from here."

"Around 9:30 should work, then," Linc decided. "I can give you directions to Gillian's or I can pick you up."

"I can drive myself," she responded quickly. She was used to standing on her own two feet and didn't want to depend on anyone, certainly not this man who was out of her league.

"All right. Do you want me to meet you there, or do you want me to stay out of it altogether? I do want you to keep in mind that Gillian and I will be discussing this even though any tips the hotline receives will be routed to the detective in charge. I never know what else might develop from airing the interview."

Work with a psychic. Just what did that entail? Linc was saying he probably had connections she'd need, so her answer was obvious. "I'd like you to be involved, but I know how busy you must be."

"Everyone is busy with what they make themselves busy with. I can clear my schedule in the morning."

"Then I really would like you there." For moral support, as well as his connections, she realized. "Would you like that coffee?"

He checked his watch. "I'd better go. I have other calls to make tonight. I'll let Gillian know we're on for the morning. She suggested you bring a picture of your sister and something personal of hers if you have it. A piece of clothing is always good...jewelry, too."

"Her clothes are here. With the close of the semester at school, she'd emptied her dorm room."

"So she lived with you when school wasn't in session?"

"Yes. And babysat for me. She's great with Becky..." Emma's voice trailed off. Then she swallowed and went on, "As I told Tessa, she'd just finished earning an associate degree and was looking for work."

Linc looked as if he wanted to console her...or something. But instead, he walked through the living room into the kitchen and then to the carport door.

Emma stepped outside with him. Night had fallen. The neighborhood was quiet except for the slam of a car door, a dog barking in the distance. Wisteria grew along the side and roof of the carport and Emma suddenly felt as if she and Linc were standing in a world of their own. The kitchen light sent a dim glow outside, but he was standing in shadow and she couldn't altogether see his face.

"Today turned out to be quite different than I expected," she told him.

He shifted toward her and she could see him more clearly. The brisk tone he'd used before was gone as he said, "The interview itself had to wear you out, let alone the stress from my suggestion. If you aren't entirely comfortable with this idea, Emma, just say so. It doesn't have to go any further."

She considered her interview, their walk on the beach and everything Linc had said. "It's been three months, Linc. The trail for the police is long dead. I can't sleep at night wondering where Paige is and what's happened to her. She's only twenty. She had her whole life in front of her."

"She might still have. That's why we're going to see Gillian."

"To get answers, one way or another," Emma concluded, not knowing if she could believe a psychic, not knowing what would happen next.

The anguish in her voice must have brought Linc closer, because suddenly he was near enough to touch and was holding onto her shoulder. "It's better to know the truth than to constantly think about the worst, don't you think?"

"Yes."

His hand slid under her hair and she could feel his

thumb on her neck and his finger almost caressed her. "Emma."

The sound of her name was a warning, telling her she should step away if she didn't want what was going to come next. But the intensity in Linc's eyes, the nerve working in his jaw, the potent attraction she'd felt from the first time she'd met him urged her to stand absolutely still. The silence between them was heart-poundingly loud. The air seemed to quiver with anticipation.

Then Linc bent his head and she lifted her chin. His mouth came down on hers with a demand that she couldn't deny. The pressure of his lips was momentary and then his tongue slipped into her mouth. She felt herself reaching for him, sliding her hand up his nape, relishing the feel of his thick, dark hair. When she melted against him, he held her tighter. She could feel his belt buckle against her midriff, feel his arousal that took her breath away. This man desired her, really desired her. The way he kissed...

...Told her he was an expert. From what she'd read, he'd never married. She hadn't dated much in high school because of her mom being sick. Caring for her and watching over Paige had taken over most waking hours. She'd met Barrett after their mom had died while she was going to school at night to earn her degree. He'd been her first and only. Lincoln Granger so outclassed her in so many ways, she'd better not get caught up in the moment or use him as an escape because of what was happening with her sister.

He must have felt her withdraw even before she actually withdrew because he ended the kiss and backed off, slowly releasing her.

She found her footing on the asphalt, composed herself as best she could before she looked up into his eyes.

"If that wasn't what you wanted, it won't happen again." His voice was just a bit husky and she was glad to hear he'd been affected by the kiss, too.

"I don't know what I want. This is a confusing time."

"I know. I certainly don't want to make it more confusing." His voice took on that brisk tone again when he said, "Let me give you Gillian's address." He took his wallet from his back pocket and slipped out a card. He was careful when he handed it to her, that their fingers didn't touch. Because if they did, they might kiss again?

"Do you need directions?" he asked.

"No, my car has a GPS."

"Good. Then I don't have to worry about you getting lost. I'll see you at Gillian's tomorrow at 9:30."

Then Linc Granger walked down her driveway to

his car, climbed inside, backed out and drove away.

Emma felt lost already.

Chapter Three

The following morning, shaken up more than he wanted to admit by last night's kiss—a woman's kiss had never done that—Linc concentrated on ringing Nathan's doorbell. He was purposefully five minutes late because he'd guessed Emma would be early. She'd be over-the-top anxious about this appointment. At least if he showed up last they wouldn't be alone together, wouldn't have to look into each other's eyes and remember that kiss.

Gillian opened the door to the two-story stucco home and smiled up at him. "Hey, Linc. Emma and I have been having a cup of coffee. Would you like some?"

"Black," he said tersely, and Gillian arched an eyebrow at him.

He knew she didn't read minds or anything like that, but sometimes her intuition was just a little too uncanny.

He followed Gillian through the foyer into the living room and there Emma was. She'd worn a peach skirt and matching tank, with white beads around her neck and white sandals on her feet. He noticed right away that her nails were painted one of those neutral shades. Remembering her fingers in his hair, he wished he hadn't noticed. He wished everything about her didn't cause a reaction in him.

Gillian went to the coffee table and poured him a mug of coffee. When she handed it to him, he mumbled, "Thanks," and sat in the wing chair beside the sofa. Practically speaking, he had to break the silence between him and Emma. "How are you this morning?"

She gave him what was supposed to pass as a smile. "Nervous."

He nodded, understanding that.

"Emma was just giving me some background," Gillian told him.

"She wanted to know about us growing up, how close Paige and I were."

Linc decided to just keep quiet and listen. He knew Emma and Gillian had to connect.

"So...you took care of Paige and essentially acted as

guardian of her after your mother died," Gillian prompted as if Linc's arrival hadn't interrupted their conversation.

"Yes. After I married, she lived with us until she went to school. Then she stayed with us on holidays and throughout summer vacation. After Barrett died, it was a comfort to have her around. She was so good with Becky."

Linc knew Gillian just wanted Emma to relax and go into stream of consciousness memories.

"She got along with your husband?"

"Oh, yes. They were like big brother and sister."

Gillian didn't miss a beat and asked next, "Can you tell me some of Paige's favorite places to go?"

"Like me, she loved the beach. She also liked hiking. Before Becky was born, the three of us would do that together. But most of all, she just liked to go any place quiet and sketch. She was quiet as a child. I think mom getting sick pushed her even deeper into herself. She'd always been artistic and was hardly ever without her sketch pad."

"So she wasn't the type who would attend frat parties and bar hop?"

"I don't know exactly what went on when she was at school, but I doubt that very much. Her artistic nature spoke loud and clear when she painted blue streaks through her hair. But that was how Paige expressed her-self—blue hair and funky clothes she designed."

"Did she date much?"

"No. One guy lasted longer than all the others, Craig Jamison. They dated for about six months. But that was almost two years ago. She broke it off with him before Barrett died. They'd had a big fight about something. She wouldn't tell me what. It was so sudden. I thought maybe he wanted to get more serious and she didn't, or vice versa. But she just wouldn't tell me. She said it was over and she was moving on and that was all that mattered."

Linc wondered if the cops had questioned Craig Jamison and what they'd decided about him, if he was a person of interest.

"Did you know this Craig well?" Gillian inquired.

"Not well but I liked him. He spent Thanksgiving and Christmas with us."

"Do you think he was the type of person who would harbor a grudge if Paige was the one who broke it off?"

"Are you asking me if I think he had something to do with her disappearance? If he did, I'm a very bad judge of character."

Linc used several means to figure out if someone was a good judge of character. He would use that litmus test here. Holding up his hand for a moment, he stopped the flow of Gillian's inquiries, and Gillian acknowledged that he wanted to break in.

"How long have you been running your business?" Linc asked Emma.

"I started it right out of business school."

"The bank gave you a loan?"

"Yes. I had a small inheritance from my mom and her life insurance. That was my collateral so to speak."

"And has your business grown in the past five years?"

"Yes. I've turned a larger profit each year. I plan to pay back the loan in two more years."

"Do you have repeat customers?"

"They're the core of my business."

"Do you have a key to your neighbor's house?"

Now she looked mildly annoyed, as if wondering what any of this had to do with why she was here. "Yes. I take care of Maris's plants when she's away, and just check on the place. She has a key to mine, too, of course, because of Becky."

"Are you still in touch with any of your friends from high school?"

Now she finally did erupt. "What does this have to do—"

He didn't get defensive because he understood Emma felt he was interrogating her, not just filling in information about Paige. "Just answer my last question."

She glanced at Gillian, then back at him. "*Yes*, I'm still in touch with two of the girls I hung around with in high school. One of them was a friend from grade school. Linc, can you tell me why you're asking me all of this?"

He leaned forward in his chair, and his gaze locked to hers unwaveringly. "First of all, you're a savvy businesswoman or you wouldn't still be in business. With the economic climate the way it's been, a bank wouldn't have given you a loan as young as you were unless you were a good risk. You have a core set of customers, who obviously like you and trust what you do. You have a neighbor who also trusts you, and you trust her. And if you've hung onto some of your high school friends, you know how to establish bonds and know how friendship can last. So as far as Craig Jamison goes, I do think you're a good judge of character. You'd have to be to live the life you're in now."

He shrugged one shoulder at Gillian.

Sitting next to Emma on the sofa, Gillian patted her hand. "Linc can be my rational side. So can my partner, Jake, and of course my husband. They're all experienced in ways I'm not and I trust their judgment. Linc was just pointing out in his way how I can trust what you say."

Emma ran her hand through her hair, pushing it

over her brow. "Linc, I'm sorry. I didn't mean to get...prickly."

"Prickly happens," he said easily, respecting the fact that Emma wasn't cowed by him like some women...that she stood up for herself even in a situation like this...*especially* in a situation like this.

"Tell me what you think Paige's most important quality is," Gillian requested.

"She's loyal," Emma answered easily. "And she's devoted to me as I am to her. I think she saw me as a second mom, not just a big sister, especially when Mom was sick."

Gillian nodded. "Okay. I might have more questions later. But how about if you show me what you brought me?"

Reaching over the arm of the sofa, Emma grabbed a bag and pulled it to her lap. She withdrew a royal blue flannel jacket with a hood. "This was—" she started.

But Gillian shook her head. "Don't tell me anything about it, not yet anyway." Gillian took it from her, laid it in her lap and held the material between her fingers and closed her eyes. After a few seconds, she opened them. "Your sister had dark brown hair, instead of blond-brown like yours, right?"

"How did you know that?"

Linc placed his hand on Emma's shoulder, as if telling her to hold the questions, at least for now.

She whispered to Linc, "I didn't show her Paige's picture yet."

Gillian smiled. "You don't have to whisper. I might have caught a glimpse of her on the news without realizing I did, but I'm just absorbing the sense that she had dark hair and dark eyes and that she liked to run."

"She did run, any chance she got. When she was home, she'd go to the high school track."

Gillian nodded. "A controlled atmosphere."

"Paige—"

Again Linc capped her shoulder and he wished he didn't have to do that, because he felt some kind of current run through him when he did. And it had nothing to do with intuition or psychic ability.

"Paige liked controlled atmospheres. Is that what you were going to say?" Gillian inquired. "She wasn't a risk taker. She liked planning and making to-do lists."

"Yes, she did," Emma said, her voice just a whisper again.

Linc knew how she felt. Sort of a little bit in awe. When Gillian got on the wave length of somebody, it was downright eerie. Or fabulous. However you wanted to look at it.

"Do you have any idea of what she was wearing the day she disappeared?"

"She always wore jeans, that kind that look like somebody took a scissors to them. And she liked beaded T-shirts. But I don't know specifically what she was wearing."

Gillian stopped fingering the jacket fabric. "Can I see her picture?"

This time, as Emma drew the photograph from her purse, Linc could see that her fingers were shaking. He so much wanted to put his arm around her, hold her hand, anything to help her feel better.

When Emma handed the photo to Gillian, she watched her expectantly.

Gillian took the photograph and studied it. "She's a beautiful young woman."

Linc noticed that she used the present tense. He wondered if that was for Emma's sake or if Gillian had a feeling that Paige was still alive. He wasn't about to bring that up or ask.

"Did you bring anything else of hers?"

Quickly Emma retrieved a small envelope and shook a necklace into her hand. It was a gold unicorn. "My mother gave her this and she usually wore it. I'm not sure why she left it behind that weekend, but she did."

Emma carefully laid the necklace into Gillian's palm. Again Gillian shut her eyes and kept them closed for a little while.

Linc saw the hope on Emma's face, and he suddenly wasn't sure he'd done the right thing by bringing her here. What if nothing came of it? Worse yet, what if the news was bad?

But after a little while, Gillian opened her eyes and just gave a slight shake of her head. "If it's all right with you, I'm just going to hold onto these things. Energy's a funny thing. There's no past, present or future with it, so I can get mixed-up messages that don't always make a lot of sense. For the next week or so, I'm just going to think about your sister, handle her things and keep a journal of all my sensations. If something specific pops up, I'll give you a call. If it doesn't, in about a week, I might ask you for a photograph album or something like that. I might want to come to your house and walk around Paige's room if that's okay with you."

"Whatever you need to do."

Gillian looked straight into Emma's eyes and said honestly, "Nothing might come of this."

"Linc told me you have a good success rate."

"Linc is a dear friend who believes in what I do. But that doesn't mean I always succeed."

Nodding, Emma stood. "Call me anytime. You have my cell number and my home phone."

Gillian rose to her feet, too, and so did Linc. He knew there was nothing more to be done today. This process took time.

Gillian held out her hand to Emma. "It was good

to meet you. I'll be in touch."

And then she walked them to the door.

Linc gave Gillian a hug and led Emma to the driveway.

They stood at her car while he vividly recalled the night before. He could tell she was remembering, too, because of the golden sparks in her very brown eyes. He'd seen those sparks last night, just before she'd closed them, just before his lips had settled on hers.

Breaking the silence, he asked, "What do you think of Gillian?"

"I like her. She's sincere and I believe she wants to help."

"But?" he prompted.

"But I know this a long shot, whether she has a good success rate or not." Emma's voice was resigned as if she'd convinced herself nothing might come of Gillian's gift.

"You do understand that her partner, Jake Donovan, will be on this too if she comes up with anything? And maybe even if she doesn't. Do you want him to go ahead and nose around?"

"I feel so guilty asking them to do this for free."

"It's what they do, Emma."

She must have heard the "you've got to believe me" tone in his voice, because she lifted her chin and said,

"This is all new to me. I don't even know these people. Yet you want me to trust them."

"Is trust hard for you?"

She seemed surprised by his question. "No. Is it hard for you?"

"Yes."

Quick on her feet, she shot back, "In general or in particular?"

"Both. So when I say I trust Gillian and Jake, just know that that trust didn't come easily. They both earned it."

Quiet now, Emma seemed to mull that over. Then she looked up at him again and those golden sparks were back. He wanted to kiss her much deeper and hotter and wetter than he'd kissed her last night.

Instead, he took a step back while she used the remote to open her car door.

"You'll call me if you hear anything?" she asked.

"Gillian will contact you if she connects in any way."

Emma looked as if she wanted to say more, yet she didn't. She slid into the driver's seat and shut her door.

Linc almost wished he'd thrown caution to the wind and kissed her again. But he never threw caution to the wind. Not ever.

The bell over the door chimed as Linc walked into *Occasional Baskets*, wishing he had good news for Emma. Maybe one of the tips generated form the hotline that had blinked across the TV screen after last night's special would pay off. All calls were being routed to the detective in charge of the case. After Emma's interview last night had aired, Linc had thought about calling her. But he hadn't. This morning, however, he'd decided to stop by her shop this evening.

The store didn't have much floor space in the strip shopping center, but he could see right away what space it had was well utilized. He noticed the pleasant scent of candles, not the over-powering heady sweetness that some shops had. There were all types of baskets in various colors, here, there and everywhere, with everything from lotions and soaps to stationery, potholders and towels. Balloons flew high above a few.

A mature redhead sat at a writing desk in one corner, a phone at her ear. Linc could hear her taking an order. Emma stood behind the cashier's desk speaking with a man who appeared to be in his fifties, with grey hair and wire rim glasses.

As he approached the counter, he heard her say, "Thanks, Earl. No more deliveries today. We'll start fresh tomorrow."

Earl adjusted his glasses. "I hope someone calls in

about Paige. You've got to believe she'll be found."

Emma and the man exchanged a few more words, then he left through the rear of the shop. Linc guessed there was storage space beyond that door and then an outside entrance.

As soon as Emma spotted him, she came around the cashier's desk toward him. "Is there any word?"

He had suspected she'd be on proverbial pins and needles. She looked tired with blue smudges under her eyes. As she settled the basket she'd been holding on the counter, he could see her hands shake. She was at the end of her rope, whether she knew it or not.

He wasn't throwing caution to the wind today by coming here. He was just checking up on her. "The cops are following any tips from the hotline and there's no word from Gillian," he said right away. "I didn't mean to scare you."

Emma put her hand to her forehead, brushing tendrils of hair away. He wanted to brush them back himself. He wanted to run his fingers through that hair again and feel its glossy softness.

"I've been so tempted to call Gillian," Emma confessed. "But I didn't know if I should."

"I'm sure she wouldn't mind you phoning. But if she had anything to tell you, believe me, she'd be calling you. I haven't talked to her because I know the way

Gillian works. Have you had anything to eat today?"

For a few moments Emma looked as if she truly didn't remember. Then she said, "Toast this morning."

"It's almost 5:00. Can you leave? We can go get dinner."

"I can leave, but...I really should get home to Becky. I put in a lot of hours this week because we were so busy."

Linc ignored the pang of disappointment. "Is there any chance you and your daughter like Chinese? There's a good place not far from here and we could take it along to your place."

"We both like Chinese, but you don't have to—"

"I know I don't have to. I want to. Unless—" He lowered his voice. "If you don't want me to come to dinner, I understand."

Maybe having him at her home once was enough. Maybe she was careful who she brought around her daughter. That's the way it should be. Maybe their kiss had fueled her reluctance to invite him in again. Who was he to impose? Except that he did want to make sure that she ate. This way he could.

"I don't mind," she finally responded, her gaze on his. "It's just...I'm not very good company right now."

Unable to resist touching her any longer, he took her hand in his. "With good reason. I don't have any expectations."

She studied his face so long and hard enough that he felt like shifting from one foot to the other. Maybe his motives weren't completely stellar, but he also in a way felt responsible for what was happening.

As if resolving something in her own mind, she gave him a bit of a smile. "Becky was asking me about you this week. She wondered if you'd visit again."

"So I made an impression?"

Now Emma's smile broke free, dazzling him. "Stop fishing for compliments. You know you did. You're obviously at home around kids and Becky could sense that. She had a good time while you were there. Let's face it, I'm not a barrel of laughs these days. I try to hide my concern and worry, but she picks it up."

"Make me a list of your favorite Chinese entrées. I'll call in the order and they'll be ready when we drive by."

"You *do* like to take charge," Emma joked.

"My worst fault," he said with a grin, and she laughed. That laugh made him feel as if he'd won the lottery.

Becky liked noodles. Linc wished he had a camera as Emma's daughter slurped them one by one, chicken lo mein being her entree of choice. Although Emma was putting on a pretense of eating, he noticed that she pushed her food around on her plate more than she ate.

He wiggled a piece of chicken at Becky that he'd dipped in sweet and sour sauce. "Are you interested? These very good nuggets are almost gone."

Becky giggled, snatched it from him and popped it into her mouth. Talking around it, she asked, "Mommy?"

"What, baby?"

"Can Linc play with me?"

Emma stopped fiddling with her food. "What would you like him to play?"

"Barbies."

Emma's smile was indulgent. "I know you'd like to play Barbies, but I'm not sure Linc would. How about a game of Candyland instead?"

Becky thought about that, apparently not happy with having her plans derailed. "Okay, if he reads a story, too."

"You'll have to ask him."

Following her mom's suggestion, Becky looked up at him, obviously seeing no sense in repeating it all. "Can we?"

"You're a real negotiator."

"What's a ne-go-shator?"

Emma responded, "It's someone who tries to get what they want, and you're good at that. Go on to the bathroom and wash your hands before you get out the game."

As Becky slid off her chair, she gave Linc a grin, then darted through the living room.

Immediately, Emma stood and began cleaning up their dishes.

Linc stayed her arm. "You didn't eat much."

"I ate. You just didn't see how much because you were talking to Becky."

Wanting to pull her close instead of letting go, he let go anyway. "You're not fooling me."

She kept her gaze averted as she told him, "I'm fine, Linc. Really." Then she said, "Trash bags are in the closet over there. Grab me one, will you? Thank goodness we used paper dishes. We can just toss it all."

He didn't step over to the closet for the trash bags. Instead, he tipped her chin up so she couldn't evade him. The moment their gazes locked, he felt the kitchen become a lot warmer. "You might be able to distract Becky, but you can't distract me."

When she didn't respond, when she just looked at him as if a distraction was what she wanted most, he kissed her.

It was quick and hard and fast, with a flourish of his tongue, and it wasn't nearly enough. But with Becky not far away, it would have to be.

"I can think of a way to distract us both, but not with a four-year-old chaperone nearby."

He saw answering sparks of desire in Emma's eyes. However, her words contradicted them. "I don't need a distraction. I need some answers."

"What if you don't get any answers?"

"I won't accept that. I'll keep calling the police, I'll keep searching the internet on my own. I will find out what happened to my sister."

"I'm ready," Becky called from the living room.

This scene looked domestic enough. After all, he was getting ready to gather up the trash. The four-year-old in the next room was beginning to like him. Although her mother wouldn't admit it, she was as attracted to him as he was attracted to her. Or was that his arrogance talking? Was he seeing something that wasn't there? Or feeling something that wasn't there?

As he turned to open the pantry door, Emma said, "Linc?" Something in her voice made him turn around again.

"I can't even consider what you're suggesting. Sometimes with Paige missing, I feel as if I shouldn't even smile. I feel guilty when I'm with Becky that I can forget for a little while—or that I can forget when you kiss me."

Ah, so that was it. Good old, make-the-world-spin guilt. He'd known his share of that. After Colleen's abortion, he'd wondered what was lacking in him that she couldn't trust him, that she couldn't have told him that she was pregnant. Maybe his arrogance had played a part in that, too, that Colleen knew he would have tried to control the situation. She would have been right.

But all he said to Emma was, "I understand guilt. But that can't keep you from experiencing happiness. Come on, let's get this cleaned up so we can enjoy some time with your daughter."

Emma looked as if she wanted to hug him, or do more, or say more. But she didn't. She just gave him one of those half-smiles of hers and went back to the table to clean up their supper.

An hour later after three games of Candyland, Linc read Becky a story. Her eyes were already starting to close as Emma took over to help her daughter get ready for bed. Linc went out to the living room, had just settled on the couch with the remote, when his cell phone rang.

When he saw Gillian's number, he answered right away. "What's going on?"

"Where are you?" Gillian's voice sounded urgent.

"I'm with Emma...at her place."

That seemed to give his friend pause, but she only waited a beat before she asked, "Do you think she'd mind if I drop over?"

Chapter Four

Linc introduced Jake Donovan to Emma as Gillian stood to one side, giving her a reassuring smile.

Emma's head began to swirl. Something was going to happen. She could feel it. Both Gillian and her partner wouldn't be here if it wasn't. Right?

The little bit she'd eaten for dinner had made her nauseous. But she ignored anything and everything except the firm grip of Jake's hand on hers and the idea that she could find Paige. Linc had done this for her and she was so grateful to him for giving her hope. He'd warned her before Gillian had arrived that this just might be about more details...but details could be everything.

Emma went to the sofa and sat down, not sure her legs were going to hold her up. Gillian sat beside her, but Linc and Jake stood, as if they were waiting for something. Jake was Linc's height, but huskier. Since he was formerly a cop, she'd expected him to be a little removed. But he didn't have the guarded look she'd seen in the detective's eyes she'd dealt with after Paige had disappeared. Maybe that was a good sign.

Gillian began. "I need to talk to you about a couple of things."

"Anything," Emma assured her.

"I spoke with Craig Jamison. I didn't get the impression he'd ever do Paige any harm. He said they broke up because she was too busy with school projects to give them much time to be together. I believe he was telling the truth. I don't think their relationship was more than friendship. So I decided to contact the detective assigned to Paige's case. He didn't tell me much, but he did say since your husband had died just a year ago, they had looked into whether his death and your sister's disappearance could be connected."

Never had anything close to that crossed Emma's mind. "You're not serious!"

"I am. But they couldn't find anything. No connection at all. But that doesn't mean there isn't one."

"How do we figure it out? His accident was one in a chain, when someone stopped suddenly on the freeway. Traffic was backed up for hours."

"They apparently took it apart, looking into every

aspect of it. But to tell you the truth, I don't get the feeling that your husband's accident had anything to do with your sister's disappearance."

If that was true, then Emma wasn't sure why Gillian was here.

"The detective pulled your sister's folder and had it on his desk. He, of course, wouldn't let me look at it. But I got this strong sensation he wasn't telling me everything. I had taken along Paige's picture and her necklace. While I was speaking with him, I got the strongest sensation that San Diego is important. Can you tell me if your sister had a connection to San Diego?"

Emma was feeling queasy again...and very tired. But this wasn't the time to be low-energy. She searched her mind for anything Paige might have said about San Diego. But she couldn't think of any reference, none at all. She shook her head.

Now Jake entered the discussion. "Did Paige have a computer?"

"She had a laptop. She took it with her when she left. When I asked the police about it, they said it could have been stolen from her car while it was sitting alongside the highway."

"And her purse?" Jake probed.

"That was gone, too."

Jake and Gillian exchanged a look that Emma

didn't understand. Then Gillian asked, "Do you have a computer?"

"Yes, in my bedroom."

"Did Paige ever use it?"

"Sure. When she didn't feel like booting up her laptop, or when her laptop froze up or crashed."

"Do you mind if I take a look at it?" Jake asked.

"No, I don't mind. What do you think you'll find?"

"Old e-mails, and maybe I can access her social networking accounts."

"Social networking? You mean like *Branches*?" Although Emma only used her computer for store-related business and some word processing—she really didn't have time for anything else—she knew about the social networking site Paige accessed on a daily basis. Her sister had wanted her to get involved, too, stating it would be good for her business. She'd even given Emma her password so Emma could fish around before deciding to do it. But Emma had just never taken the time to explore, let alone set up an account.

Linc explained, "*Branches, Facebook, Twitter.* Women your sister's age do a lot of that," he said, with half of a smile.

"As well as texting," Jake added. "But I accessed your sister's phone records and its use stopped the day she disappeared. I'm sure the detective on the case did the same thing and checked the numbers for the past few months. I didn't find anything unusual, but there are a couple of her friends that I'd like to interview if you think they'd be willing."

"I can call them."

"I'm bringing Jake in on this," Gillian said, "because his skill set is different than mine."

"I do the hard-assed investigative work," he said wryly, and Gillian made a face at him.

Linc asked Emma, "Are your computer accounts password protected?"

"The passwords are automatically saved so I don't have to look them up each time."

"Not a good idea," Jake told her, shaking his head. "That's what most people do. But it's a security nightmare."

"Come on. I'll show you where it is," Emma offered, rising to her feet, feeling a little hazy as she did. She only managed a few hours of sleep each night and she was just tired. That's all.

"We'll be quiet so we don't wake your daughter," Jake told her. "Linc said she was already in bed for the night."

"She's a sound sleeper. Once she's asleep, she's usually out until around 7:00 a.m."

Gillian rose, too. "You are *so* lucky. Matthew wakes

up if I tiptoe across the carpet. Sometimes I think he's just waiting for us to make a noise so he can call out for us, thinking he's going to play. *I* put him back to bed. Nathan—he says that that's their guy time—and he plays with him when he wakes up. In the middle of the night! He just hates to see Matthew's crocodile tears."

"That's Nathan. A softie," Linc dead-panned.

He followed them into Emma's bedroom and she wondered what he thought. There was a double bed, a dresser with a mirror, a chest and a computer hutch. The room was neither masculine nor feminine. There were lots of stripes in green-and-navy with beige Berber carpeting. Barrett had chosen the heavy pine furniture and she'd decorated with his tastes in mind. She hadn't wanted to change anything after he died. It had taken her a few months just to give his clothes to Goodwill. She still grieved for her husband. But now when she looked at the room she thought maybe she should have made some changes, maybe she should have been trying harder to move on.

As Jake sat at the computer chair, Gillian stood looking over his shoulder.

"The printer is hooked up to the computer?" Jake asked.

"Yes. Print out anything you need to."

"This is going to take a while," Jake explained. "If you'd rather wait in the living room, that's fine."

"No. I want to see what you're doing. I want to see...everything about my sister."

Suddenly Linc was beside her. Taking her by the hand, he led her over to the bed. There was a chest at the foot of it and they sat on that, side by side, his expensive suit trousers brushing her jeans. This whole scene seemed so unreal, and she felt a little disoriented.

"Are you okay?" he asked, still holding her hand.

She liked the feel of his large, warm hand around hers, the texture of his skin against hers. But she fought against that comforting feel. "I'm fine." She drew her hand away.

Why couldn't she lean into him and just enjoy his protective concern? Because she was still grieving? Because her sister had disappeared? Because she had a daughter to raise, and she had to focus her attention on Becky?

Jake and Gillian went at it for over an hour. They worked in a coordinated effort, as if they had done this many times before. Jake found e-mails related to Paige and while Gillian read them in one window, Jake opened another, searching and searching and searching. They asked Emma questions about names and places they found. Emma thought she had known all of Paige's friends, but when Jake switched to *Branches* and other social networking sites, she realized she hadn't known everyone Paige was connected to.

Linc said to her more than once, "Not everybody is a real friend. People hook up on these sites because they're interested in the same subjects, share thoughts about celebrities, movies and books."

Jake had printed out pages and pages for Gillian to sort through, too, and the printer ran out of paper.

Emma was glad for something to do. "I keep the reams in the hall closet. I'll get more." She needed a break from her closeness to Linc. She needed to take a few deep breaths. Air suddenly seemed to be at a premium.

She kept the box of paper on the floor in the closet. She bought it in bulk because that was more economical, and when she was doing bookwork she liked a hard copy to look over, too.

After she opened the closet, she stooped over to pull the heavy box from under the bottom shelf. She did, flipped the lid off and lifted out a ream of paper. But when she stood, everything was grey. Dots danced in front of her eyes and her ears rang. She thought the sensation would pass, but suddenly she felt clammy and disoriented. When she grabbed for the door handle, it slipped from her hand.

She felt herself falling...falling...falling...then closed her eyes as all the little black spots became one huge black curtain that surrounded her right before she passed out.

When Emma awakened she was lying on her sofa, a cool cloth across her forehead and one at the back of her neck. The first thing she thought was that the pillow in back of her head was going to get wet. Then she opened her eyes and saw Linc. He was kneeling on the floor beside the sofa, his hand on that cool washcloth. Gillian and Jake were standing nearby.

"Don't tell me you're fine," Linc scolded her. "Does anything hurt? I shouldn't have moved you, but I just scooped you up—"

He'd carried her to the sofa? She almost smiled at the image that presented. But then it all came rushing back and she knew she shouldn't be smiling at all. "I just bent over for the paper and when I went to straighten up, everything got fuzzy. She started to sit up. "But I'm really—" She stopped. From the stormy look in his eyes, she knew she'd better not say it.

"I called a friend of mine. He's a doctor. He's going to stop by."

"Linc, that's unnecessary. Two of your friends are already here. Do you really think you need reinforcements?" She was trying to make light of this but not doing a very good job.

"I want Zack to check you over. I already told him

you're not eating much and you're not sleeping."

"Oh, thank you. That will give him a great impression of my life."

"Emma. If you don't take care of yourself, how will you take care of Becky? Stop being obtuse about this."

"Obtuse?" She snuck a look at him. "What kind of doctor is this Zack?"

"His specialty is internal medicine. Fainting isn't anything to fool around with."

"I didn't faint. I was just a little dizzy."

"You passed out *cold*."

Ever since she'd known Linc, she hadn't seen him look angry, but he looked angry now.

"How many friends do you have?" she asked. "I don't think my house is big enough for them all."

Finally his expression gentled, and he relented a little. "I meet a lot of people in my business. I met Zack when he was just an intern. At that time hospital shows were in and I was taping some real life segments to use for research. He and I got to talking and we've been friends since."

"Does he still work at a hospital?"

"No. He has a private practice. But he's thinking about taking a break from it all for a while."

"Why?"

"That's his story to tell. But he's known tragedy

and it's affected him. He's always thinking about jumping on his motorcycle and taking off for parts unknown."

If she kept talking and kept Linc talking, he wouldn't look so worried. "Which parts?"

"I don't think he cares. But he's good with horses. His parents owned a ranch when he was growing up. They had to sell it because times just got too tough, but I think it's always been a second love of his."

Gillian handed Emma a glass of juice. "Drink this. You could be dehydrated."

Emma sighed, took the juice and drank it. Then she said, "Please don't hover. Go back to what you were doing."

After Gillian gave Linc a long look, he nodded. Jake and Gillian disappeared into the bedroom once more.

Linc wouldn't let Emma move from the sofa until Zack arrived. He entered her house carrying a doctor's bag and she felt foolish all over again.

After Linc introduced Zack to Emma, he said to his friend, "Make her tell you what she's eaten in the past week. It wouldn't even fill one of your pill bottles." To Emma, he asked, "Do you want me to send Gillian in to watch out for you while Zack examines you?"

Dr. Zackary Burke had black hair and blue eyes

and looked as if he could be a heartbreaker. But there was something in those blue eyes that told Emma he *did* need a break. Maybe because she'd just found out she wasn't Superwoman and had limits, she could see his. "I don't need Gillian. Let her work."

Zack didn't try to make small talk, simply asked her questions about diet and exercise. He took her blood pressure and listened to her heart. He put a strip on her forehead to take her temperature, tested her reflexes and then looked into her throat. He had a gentle, caring touch—not at all like some doctors who rushed through an exam as if their patient was a mannequin.

Zack asked her about aches and pains and headaches and insomnia. She answered truthfully on all accounts. When he was finished, he pulled a hassock up in front of the sofa and sank down onto it.

Giving her a penetrating glare meant to be stern, he said, "You have to take better care of yourself."

She'd heard this from Linc, but having a doctor say it to her shook her up. "That's difficult when I have no appetite and I'm worried every minute of the day."

The look in his eyes softened along with his voice. "Linc told me what's going on and I understand. But you have to manage to grab time for yourself. You have to figure something out so that you relax or exercise or both at least a half hour a day—better yet twice a day—in addition to eating the right food and keeping yourself hydrated. Cut caffeine out of your vocabulary. I want to make sure nothing sinister is going on, so I'd like you to have some blood work done tomorrow. Will you?"

"Yes."

"You'll have to fast for ten hours. And I'm going to leave sleeping medication to help straighten out your sleep cycle."

As his blue eyes kept clinically assessing her, he took off his stethoscope and pushed it into his bag on the coffee table.

"Can I ask you something?" Emma needed more information where Linc was concerned.

"You can ask."

"Why did you do this for Linc tonight?"

Obviously reluctant to answer, Zack finally responded, "Linc has been around when I needed him."

"And you've been around for him," she guessed.

Smiling for the first time since he arrived, Zack stood. "Are you trying to figure him out?"

She felt herself blush. "Maybe I am. He just kind of jumped into my life and—"

Now Zack's smile was a full-fledged grin. "He can be a bit overwhelming, but Linc's intentions are usually good."

"Just usually?" Linc asked from the hall doorway, obviously hearing at least part of their discussion.

Trying to recover her composure from everything that had happened, Emma finally rose from the couch.

"So what caused the fainting?" Linc asked Zack.

"My hunch is—low blood sugar. But you had already guessed that. The best thing you can do for her—" At Emma's raised brows, he amended, "The best thing she can do for herself is warm up something to eat and get a good night's sleep. If the dizziness happens again, I'll set up some other tests. She'll have blood work in the morning."

"You'll still be around to give me the results?" she asked.

Zack shot a look at Linc. "I'll be around for another few weeks."

Then the handsome doctor made sure everything was where it should be in his bag, clicked it shut, and left.

Linc wrapped his arm around Emma's waist, and this time she didn't protest or pull away. He was tall and hard and solid and everything she seemed to need right at the moment.

"How do Chinese leftovers sound?"

"I think I'd rather have peanut butter toast."

He arched his brows at her, then shrugged. "Peanut butter toast it is."

Linc wasn't sure what was happening to him. When he'd seen Emma crumple to the floor, he'd felt absolute panic. He never panicked. He couldn't in his business, with the world and finances and ratings changing from minute to minute. If he didn't have something planned, he winged it and not much ruffled him.

But seeing Emma fall to the floor had.

While the bread toasted, he poured two glasses of milk. As she slathered peanut butter on the toast and then ate her snack, they talked. Granted, he was trying to distract her while Jake and Gillian did their thing. But the talking led him to a deeper appreciation of Emma and her life, though he didn't give away a whole lot about his.

At least he didn't until she asked, "So what was your childhood like? I told you all about mine and how I want Becky's to be better and different. But I want to know something about Linc Granger, the kid."

A smudge of peanut butter on her upper lip had him reaching toward her before he could help himself. He wiped it away with his thumb. Her gaze took on that deer-in-the-headlights fascination with his and they simply stared at each other for a very long time.

"Was that meant to derail me from taking the conversation any further?" she finally asked as he leaned back in his chair.

"Maybe."

"Just maybe?"

She hadn't known him very long and already she could see through him. That was scary. He thought he did a very good job of covering whatever he didn't want anyone else to know.

"If you don't want to tell me, that's fine. But don't act as if I didn't ask the question or as if it's not important," she scolded.

"You see too much," he said brusquely.

She shrugged. "Well, perhaps the women in your life up until now just haven't delved deeper than the rich successful producer."

"You're too young to be so wise."

She laughed. "I'm not that young."

"I have ten years on you."

"You're thirty-six?"

He nodded, then couldn't stop himself before he asked, "How old was your husband?"

"He was two years older than I am."

"I feel like I'm *twenty* years older than you," Linc admitted.

"Why?"

"Because you still see the world as you want it to be, rather than as it is."

"How can you know that?"

He covered her hand with his and rubbed his

thumb across her wrist. "Just from things you say. You're not jaded, Emma. You don't have an edge. You're honest with people and expect them to be honest with you in return."

"So you think I can't see reality as it is?"

"I don't think you *want* to see reality as it is."

Frowning, she pulled her hand away. "You're so wrong. After Barrett died, I had no choice but to face reality. I had Becky to raise on my own. I made my business more successful with sheer determination and hard work. That's facing reality."

Apparently she'd taken his comments as insults. "I meant all of those things that I said as a compliment."

She took a sip of her milk and eyed him. "Really?"

"Really," he assured her.

After another sip of milk, she studied him until he felt uncomfortable. "What?"

"I don't think you're as jaded as *you* think you are. I think you want to believe in the best even if you see the worst. Why did you decide to help me?"

"Because I saw a good story." He wasn't going to put a pretty picture on it for her.

"You felt no compassion for what I was going through?"

"Emma—"

"So...tell me about your childhood."

Leaning back in his chair, he realized she wasn't going to let this go. Why should she? He'd kissed her and was thinking about doing it again. "There's not much to tell. My parents were divorced. Both my parents wanted custody and I felt like a pawn. Maybe that's why I became so determined to control my own destiny."

"Who did you end up living with?"

Linc felt as if he was excavating his childhood and didn't like doing it. "My mom. But she didn't really want me. She just wanted the child support. So when I was sixteen, I went to live with my dad."

"Where's your dad now?"

"He lives in Portland."

"And your mom?"

There Emma went again, hitting a vulnerable spot. "After I went to live with Dad, she wanted nothing to do with me."

"You still don't talk?"

"Talk? All my mother cares about is money. When I was nominated for my first Emmy she contacted me wanting some."

"What did you do?"

"I gave it to her in the form of a trust she couldn't blow all at once. I haven't heard from her since."

"Oh, Linc."

The empathy in Emma's eyes was almost too much to

gaze at. The expression on her face wasn't pity, but rather understanding. He almost wanted to get up and leave. Whatever was happening between him and Emma was happening way too fast. He knew she wasn't ready for it.

What about him? He didn't know if he was ready, either. But he did know this beautiful woman with the little girl and understanding heart and too much on her plate couldn't keep handling all of it alone.

"You need to get a good night's sleep."

She laughed. "It's already midnight."

"I know. So some deep, unworried sleep matters even more."

"What are you suggesting?"

"I'm suggesting I sleep on your couch tonight. What if you get dizzy again and you're alone here with Becky? Until you have that blood work done, you won't know if something's going on that shouldn't be. Zack can probably get it rushed through. If you go to the medical center first thing in the morning, you'll know by the next day."

"Fainting won't happen again. I was just over-wrought and overtired."

"My point exactly. If I sleep on your couch, maybe you'll feel safe and actually fall into a deep sleep. When Becky gets up, I can make breakfast and you can sleep a little later."

"Absolutely not! I'm not going to start depending on you, Linc. That won't be good for me."

He was about to argue when Gillian came into the kitchen, looking excited.

"Are you sure your sister never mentioned San Diego?"

Since Emma had eaten and had lots to drink—Linc kept pushing milk and juice—she definitely felt more clear-headed, though her anxiety level hadn't lessened. She searched her mind again for any references Paige had ever made to San Diego and still came up empty.

"I'm sorry. Nothing I can remember."

Gillian pulled out a kitchen chair and sat. "Jake found posts by a man—Tim Levine."

Again, Emma searched her mind for that name, and finally shook her head.

"He and Paige had a get-to-know-you back-and-forth about a year and a half ago," Gillian said. "Then just a post here and there until another flurry about six months ago. Yet I got the sensation that they communicated in between somehow. When I read his posts, I'm getting a strong sense of Paige—like they're still very connected. Does she have a long tunic top with a tie-dye design?"

Emma felt excitement she hadn't experienced since her sister disappeared. "Yes. She made it last year for Christmas."

"That's when their posts were more frequent," Gillian murmured with a nod.

"What were they about?"

"Nothing helpful. But I got the feeling they might have taken their friendship offline. There was an email in your recycle bin from him. She thanked him for being there and said she'd call soon. When we checked this guy's stats, we saw he lived in San Diego. Jake always tries to find a fact to confirm my feeling. We did."

"So what's next?" Linc asked.

Emma had already realized he was a man of action.

Jake entered the kitchen then, looking tired, but pleased they had a lead. "Gillian and I are going to fly to San Diego. The question is—do you want to come along?"

Chapter Five

"You made a good decision," Linc said with a smile as Emma walked into the living room, carrying two pillows and a sheet.

He took them from her and somehow transferring bed pillows from her arms to his caused her racing thoughts to speed up into super-drive. This could be *such* a big mistake. "All three of you convinced me. I do need to get some rest. Tomorrow I'll have to put some things in order if we're leaving for San Diego the following morning."

"You just wanted to shut us all up. That's why you agreed to me staying. Jake and Gillian are worried about you, too," he said more softly.

"I understand. I scared everyone. They won't want me along if I can't hold my own."

After plumping the pillows, Linc plopped them at

the foot of the sofa. Then he unfurled the sheet and draped it at the opposite end.

"You're going to be uncomfortable out here. You're welcome to sleep in the guest bedroom."

"But it's really not a guest bedroom, is it? It's Paige's room."

The night had been one surprise after another. Now here she was with a near-stranger in her living room and he was spending the night.

"How am I going to explain you to Becky?" she suddenly wondered.

The look in Linc's eyes as he approached her caused Emma's breath to hitch. He was in her house, under her roof and anything could happen. But she had a daughter to think of and it couldn't.

Almost tenderly, he slid a hand on either side of her face and held her there, gazing at her with concern and desire and protectiveness she'd never felt from a man before. "Becky has sleep-overs, doesn't she?" he asked.

"You mean with friends?"

"Sure. Jake's little boy does it. Nathan's girls do, too. Just tell Becky you and I are having a sleep-over."

"I can imagine her telling that to her friends!"

Her expression must have been so wry, Linc laughed. "She'll be having a sleep-over with Maris," he pointed out reasonably.

She had to call Maris in the morning to make sure she was available to stay with Becky.

They had decided to keep their tickets open-ended. Jake would be making reservations today. So she didn't know exactly when they'd be back. She hoped she'd be back the same day. But it depended if their leads were really leads. A name from *Branches* and one email didn't seem to be much to go on.

Before Linc could kiss her and she fell into his arms, possibly ending up in her bedroom, she backed away.

"Are you going to take the sleep medication Zack left for you?" He stuffed his hands in his trouser pockets, as if he wanted to do something else with them but wasn't.

"I'd rather not. I'm tired enough. I should be able to fall asleep."

"I'm sure you've been tired other nights. Did you sleep then?"

"No," she admitted. "That's what started this whole cycle."

"Then don't try to be an iron maiden. Do what you have to do. That's why I'm staying over."

His chiding tone rubbed her the wrong way. He must have seen that because he massaged the back of his neck. "It's your life. You do what you want. I'm going to switch on the sports channel for a while if it won't bother you. And then I'm out. It takes me about two seconds to fall asleep."

Relaxing a bit, she knew he was being kind. And she was acting like a woman who— Who'd never had a man around before. That wasn't true. But her relationship with Barrett had never been filled with all these sparks...a push-pull she didn't understand...and an innate desire on her part to make sure Linc knew where she stood.

"What time do you get up?"

"Early," he said almost curtly and she felt bad that this "awkwardness" was interfering with what could be a decent friendship.

"I'll have to make some early calls and video-conference," he added.

"You won't have to go into work?"

"I'll drive into the studio tomorrow afternoon. I have a few meetings and a schedule to rearrange if I'm going to be away. I should be back for an important taping on Monday. But we'll see how things go. We don't know what we're going to find. Sometimes Jake and Gillian have to do the footwork without the well-meaning interference from relatives or friends."

"You're saying I could get in the way."

"Possibly."

There was that blunt honestly again that she wasn't sure she liked. But there were so many other things about Linc Granger that she *did* like. Maybe too many things. She'd only known the man a little over a week but it felt like a lot longer.

As Emma turned toward the hall and her bedroom, Linc asked, "Am I making you uncomfortable because you don't want me here? Or am I making you uncomfortable because you want your husband here?"

How would Barrett have acted if he were here and Paige had disappeared? She hadn't stopped to think about that. To her dismay, she realized she'd have to be taking care of him as well as Becky. After Becky had been born, he'd been...jealous of his daughter and the fact that Emma no longer had as much time to spend with him as she had before their baby had come into the world. In some ways, he'd acted entitled to what she could provide as a wife. But then they'd developed a rhythm. He'd understood Becky's needs had had to come first. Their marriage had settled into something satisfying if not exciting.

But he wouldn't have been any kind of help in this situation. Not knowing how much comfort he would have been made her sad.

"I'm confused about a lot right now, Linc. But as far as tonight goes, I'm glad you're here."

Then she hightailed it out of the living room for her bedroom before anything happened between them she'd regret.

Linc felt the tug on his arm and instantly came awake. Becky's dark brown eyes held questions and he didn't have most of the answers.

"Mommy's door's shut! Her door's not ever shut."

Linc had closed Emma's bedroom door last night after she'd fallen asleep. He'd guessed she probably left it open so she'd hear her daughter. But last night she'd needed sleep and he had intended to take care of Becky if she called.

"Your mommy's been really tired lately. So I thought it was a good idea if I stayed and helped if either of you needed anything."

Becky shifted a small pink blanket she'd dragged in over her arm and bit her lower lip as she considered his explanation. Then she eyed the remote on the coffee table. "Can we watch SpongeBob?"

Maybe Emma didn't let her watch TV in the morning. If so, today was going to be an exception. He sat up and handed her the remote. "Do you know the channel?"

Grinning at him, she pressed the "Power" button then three of the numbers.

Kids today, he thought with a shake of his head. SpongeBob popped up on the screen. At least it wasn't another Barbie movie like Nathan's youngest daughter insisted on watching.

When Becky sidled close to Linc and laid her head against his chest, then poked her thumb into her mouth, he felt as if he'd dropped into a life that wasn't really his. Draping his arm around Becky, he watched the cartoon with her.

After about a half hour, though, he'd had enough. Action was his strong suit. "Are you hungry?"

"Is there time for pancakes?"

Linc imagined that on days when Emma left for work, pancakes weren't on the breakfast menu. But today, he wasn't going to deny this little girl anything.

A few minutes later, Linc realized that Emma kept an organized pantry. It wasn't long before he found an electric griddle, pancake mix, milk and eggs.

When Becky wandered into the kitchen, her pink blanket over her arm, she pushed one of the kitchen chairs over beside him.

After she climbed up on it, she announced, "Mommy lets me watch."

"Does she let you help stir? I can always use help stirring."

Becky finally let her blanket drop to the chair seat,

took hold of the spoon he held out to her, and tried her best to stir the eggs into the mix with the milk. There were a few splashes of course. He'd have to change his shirt before he dropped by his office. But a few dollops of pancake batter were nothing compared to the good feeling in his chest for helping this mother and daughter.

He'd flipped the last of the golden brown pancakes on the griddle and was watching the scrambled eggs on the stove when Emma came through the living room. Just awakened, she looked sexy. Visions of her waking up beside him urged his internal temperature up a few degrees.

Becky must have heard her mom's soft footsteps, because from her shotgun position at the griddle, she turned and spotted her. Quicker than lightning could strike, she was off the chair and running to her.

Emma hugged her as if she hadn't seen her for a week. "Hey, baby. What are you doing?"

"Makin' us breakfast. Helpin' Linc. It's almost done. Come see."

Becky grabbed her mom's hand and pulled her toward Linc.

Emma's gaze met Linc's. "Good morning."

"Good morning to you," he said as casually as he could manage. She looked fabulous in drawstring pink patterned pants and a pink tank. He figured they were a sleeping set. Was her favorite color pink? She looked more tempting in that outfit than any woman would look in lingerie.

Had he just seen too many women in lingerie?

She pointed to the blobs of pancake batter on his shirt. "I can see Becky was helping?"

He chuckled. "How do you know I didn't do this myself?"

"Well, if you did, then I'd say the next time you should borrow my apron."

"The next time?" He picked up on that right away.

"Just a turn of phrase," she responded lightly with a slight blush, moving toward the refrigerator.

Becky had wandered with her blanket back into the living room to watch TV. So he said, "That came out a little too easily. Maybe you don't mind having a man sleeping on your couch."

"Maybe I didn't mind having you sleep on my couch. Thank you, Linc. That was the best night's sleep I've had in months."

He couldn't say he wished he'd been beside her in bed to watch her sleep, could he?

Her thoughts seemed to follow his because her cheeks seemed to pinken even more and she looked away.

"How do you feel?" he asked.

"Not dizzy. But I know I have to have that blood work done this morning. So I guess I can't eat any of this breakfast. Zack said I had to fast for ten hours."

Linc swore. "I'm sorry. I wasn't thinking."

She shook her head. "It's okay. Becky will love the pancakes. And I love leftover pancakes. When I get back, I'll warm them in the microwave." She came toward him and then laid her hand on his arm. "I'm grateful, Linc. For everything you've done. Don't ever think I'm not."

Unable to keep from putting thought into action, he wrapped an arm around her, pulled her toward the cover of the pantry closet and brought her close. Before he even considered what he was about to do, he kissed her.

When Emma's hands slid across his nape, he almost closed the pantry door. But he knew he couldn't. He also knew the kiss couldn't last too long or he'd have her clothes off as well as his. He let his tongue sweep her mouth. He let his hands roam down her back. He tortured himself with the idea of burying himself in her. Then he ended the kiss, and he merely held her.

Resting his forehead against hers, he said, "I don't want gratitude."

After a moment in which she obviously composed herself, she asked, "What *do* you want, Linc?"

On the spot, he asked himself the same question. An affair? A one-night stand? A family of his own?

Where had *that* thought come from? He willed himself to slow everything down. He tried to erect again the walls that Emma and her story had torn down. He attempted to distance himself at least for now.

"I want to find your sister for you. Or at the least, help Gillian and Jake do it. So I decided to charter a jet to fly to San Diego. There's a company I use that will accommodate us."

Emma looked as if she'd just been plunged from one world into another, and he knew the feeling. The haze of their desire could block out everything else...could let them escape...could possibly create something new. But now wasn't the time. She knew it, too.

"After breakfast, I'll make some calls," he assured her. "If we have our own plane, we won't have to waste hours in the airport, and I can get you home to Becky as soon as possible. Is that all right with you?"

He knew he couldn't just make unilateral decisions, although that was what he was used to doing most. Emma wasn't the type of woman who liked to be left out of decision-making.

"That would be the most practical thing to do," she

said, and he couldn't tell if her voice trembled a bit...if the kiss had meant something to her...if she was looking for *more* than an escape.

Maybe if they found answers in San Diego, he'd find out.

Parked at the curb in the driver's seat in one of San Diego's residential neighborhoods the following day, Linc glanced over at Emma. Her gaze was riveted to Gillian and Jake who were walking up the path to a stone and stucco rancher. They'd checked in at their hotel, one where Linc often stayed, then driven to this neighborhood not far from the college area. The city contained more than a hundred neighborhoods and had often been called the City of Villages. Mesas and canyons, agricultural preserves and business centers defined community planning areas with distinct neighborhoods. Tim Levine's neighborhood was older, but well kept. Bougainvillea climbed the trellis beside the carport. A palm tree in the front yard partially obstructed their view of the small porch and the front door of the house the man rented.

"Do you think he'll tell them anything?" Emma asked, glancing at Linc then back at Gillian and Jake.

Emma had seemed withdrawn on the plane, definitely had been lost in her thoughts. He knew she wasn't going to be able to live her life again until she found out what had happened to her sister.

"It depends where the interview goes. If he won't even let Gillian and Jake inside, they're not going to get very far. On the other hand, Gillian might be able to pick something up even if he doesn't want to talk."

"Is Jake sure he's not married?"

"He couldn't find anything. The good thing is he didn't find anything else negative, either."

"You consider being married a negative?" Emma asked.

He gave her a wry grimace. "Not what I meant. Though it is a negative if he's involved with Paige."

"Involved?"

"That's what Jake and Gillian are going to find out. I know this is tough for you." He reached over and took her hand. "But this is the first decent lead we've had."

"But you think the police already questioned him."

"If they went through Paige's *Branches* posts like we did, I'm sure they did. That's why Gillian picked up the San Diego connection from the detective."

"This is such a long shot," Emma said on a released breath.

"It is, but it's the only one we've got."

"He's opening the door." Emma's voice was tight with anxiety and excitement.

From their vantage point, Linc and Emma watched the interchange at the door. Linc's heart was beating fast so he could only imagine the speed of Emma's. You never knew in a situation like this what could happen.

Levine, who was tall and slim and wearing horned-rimmed glasses, shook his head and attempted to close his door. But Jake was quick...and strong. He held it open. Linc saw Gillian put her hand on Jake's elbow. Then she reached out and handed Levine something. But it fell to the ground. After Levine stooped over to pick it up, Gillian tapped it.

"She's trying to make contact," Linc murmured.

"Make contact?"

"Touch him in some way...or at least touch the same thing he's touching."

They saw how Jake backed off now...how Gillian shook the man's hand. Then the two of them turned away from the door and started back to the SUV.

Linc had made sure they'd rented a vehicle with darkly-tinted windows, just in case they needed some anonymity. Now he was glad of that. Levine hadn't seen him or Emma. And that might come in handy. He and Jake would have to come up with Plan B if this didn't work. Linc *always* had a Plan B.

Jake and Gillian climbed into the back of the SUV. Linc asked, "Anything?"

"Not much," Jake muttered.

"He's probably going to watch out the window until we leave," Linc concluded. "So let's get out of here."

He started up the SUV, pulled out on to the street and drove away from the house. Afterward Linc glanced in the rear view mirror at Gillian. She looked troubled.

"Let's go back to the hotel and get something to eat. We can talk there about all of this. Gillian, are you all right?"

"I'm fine," she said in a low voice.

But Linc knew something was up.

Emma must have realized it, too, because she turned around and looked at Gillian. "What did you see?"

"I'm trying to piece it together. Give me a little time to process, okay?"

Emma gave Linc a look that said—What choice did she have?

The hotel had an old-world feel with its gas light lanterns, ornate portico and tall rose bushes. "There's an outdoor cafe," Linc suggested as he handed his keys to the valet. "We can grab a table."

"Privacy is probably best," Jake decided as he glanced at Gillian. "My room or yours?" he asked Linc.

"My suite has a table large enough for a board meeting. We can spread out, talk, use the computer, do whatever we need to do."

"But my TV's bigger than yours," Jake said with an attempt at levity.

Jake and Gillian sometimes traveled on a shoestring. This time Linc was paying. They hadn't wanted a suite, so Linc had reserved the best single rooms in the hotel for each of them. "Enjoy it while you can," Linc joked back. "I don't think Sara will let you move one in that's that big." Jake's wife, Sara, was all about what was best for their son, Christopher. Like Emma, she didn't want him watching too much TV...or thinking he could have a movie theater in his house.

The women remained silent during this back and forth. But Linc knew the same thing was on all of their minds.

They rode the elevator in silence, then he used his key card to open the door. He let all three of them precede him inside. But when Emma passed him, he had to take in a big gulp of air. She was wearing sea green Capri pants and a matching top. Her perfume was a scent that was ethereally light. He wanted to wipe her worry away and give her back her life. Maybe this was a start.

Ignoring the grandeur of the living room with its gas fireplace, he went to the kitchen and pulled bottles of water and soda from the stocked refrigerator. After he set them on the table, they all took seats on the padded, cushy dining chairs. But nobody seemed interested in comfort. All eyes turned to Gillian.

Emma broke the silence. "Don't be afraid to say anything in front of me, Gillian...whether it's right or wrong or somewhere in between. I just need to know something."

"I believe Paige is alive."

Linc heard Emma's small gasp, and he leaned forward slightly to watch Gillian's expression.

"I could see Paige's name all around Tim Levine."

"He had a throw-away phone," Jake said. "When he stooped over to pick up Gillian's card, it practically fell out of his pocket. Maybe they had conversations after they met, but my guess is that it won't do any good to access his phone records to figure out what's happening now."

"He's communicating with someone on that phone," Gillian said. "Either Paige or someone else who knows where Paige is." Her voice was sure and Linc didn't doubt Gillian's vibes.

"Like a kidnapper?" Emma asked.

"Possibly," Jake responded. "But as you said, you haven't received a ransom note...no call demanding money. So either someone is holding Paige against her will or she did run away, wanting to leave her life behind."

Emma studied Gillian. "Do you know?"

"I don't know anything for certain. I'm just getting some strange signals I don't understand. From Paige's jewelry you gave me as well as from Tim Levine. It feels like...a secret of some kind."

"Between them?" Linc asked.

"No. No...and that's what's confusing."

"So Levine knows where she is?" Emma asked.

Gillian shook her head. "I can't tell you that, Emma. That's what I mean about everything being confusing. Paige might be in contact with him, but he might not know where she is. Or someone who's holding her might be in contact with him. And he still might not know."

"Why hasn't he talked to the authorities?" Emma asked almost rhetorically.

Gillian shook her head.

Linc could see Emma's frustration and it compounded his own. He said, "Why don't you and Gillian order room service? It doesn't matter what you get. Jake and I are going to conference.

"About?" Emma asked. "Don't you think I should be involved?"

"I don't want to bring you personally into this unless I have to," Linc said. "Just in case there's some kind of criminal element involved. You have to think of Becky, too."

"Of course, I'm thinking of Becky," Emma said hotly. "I can't just sit by."

"Order room service," Linc repeated. "You have to trust me."

She crossed her arms over her chest and stared him down. She was good with that because she'd had lots of practice with a four-year-old. But he was better. He *never* blinked.

He wasn't sure what he saw in her eyes eventually—it might have been resignation more than trust—but she gave in. "All right." She was saying the words but she didn't mean them because nothing was all right. "Conference with Jake," she told him curtly. "But then tell me what we're going to do next."

He didn't reply. He didn't know if he was going to tell her what they were going to do next. That all depended on what Jake thought of his idea.

In Linc's bedroom with the door closed, Jake said, "She's upset."

"Do you think I don't *know* that?" Linc asked almost angrily.

"Whoa! You've got to keep a cool head. You know that. This isn't like you."

No, this wasn't like him at all. He felt as if he'd tumbled down the proverbial rabbit hole and couldn't figure which way was out...or if he even wanted to get out. He blew out one very long breath, rubbed the back of his neck and asked his friend, "What's Gillian holding back?"

"I don't know that she is."

"Oh, yes, you do. You've been around her a lot more than I have and I know she's not telling us something."

"Maybe she doesn't feel it's time."

"I know what Emma is imagining. Someone is holding Paige and doing terrible things to her. We have to figure this out and fast."

"You sound as if you have a plan."

"I do. I want you to tail Levine tonight."

"What if he stays in all night watching TV?"

"Not likely from his posts on his *Branches* page. He seems to favor private clubs. You know that as well as I do. I want him out and about alone, someplace where I can approach him."

"Linc, I don't think this is a good idea."

"I think I can get through to him. I've gotten to know Emma, and if he cares at all about Paige, he might care about her sister, too."

"And what if he's mixed up in something shady?"

"Then you'll have my back. I'm not carrying. I guess you are."

Jake's lack of response told him he was right.

"Tail him and then call me. I'm not leaving San Diego without answers."

Jake's eyes were worried. "I hope you know what you're doing because if you mess this up, Emma's never going to forgive you."

If he messed this up...he was never going to forgive himself.

Chapter Six

After Jake and Gillian left Linc's suite, Emma called Becky. She couldn't wait to talk to her daughter, though she was concerned Becky would want her there, not here, and she'd feel even more torn up than she felt now.

But Becky seemed to be having a blast with Maris. "We went for ice cream, watched Barbie and had hot dogs with French fries!"

Becky's enthusiasm buoyed Emma and she was so relieved that her daughter didn't seem to miss her. "So what are you and Maris going to do tonight?"

"Look at my American Girl doll book."

Becky had wanted an American Girl doll for the past few months, but the expense wasn't something Emma could justify. By Christmas the doll might be a possibility. "Then what?" Emma prompted.

"Read ten books and count stars."

Counting the stars was Becky's favorite bedtime ritual. Usually by the time they'd counted twenty or so, her daughter's eyes were already closed.

"Sounds like a plan. If you keep busy with Maris, I might be home before you know it. I'll call you again in the morning, and maybe we can have breakfast together, long distance style. You can slurp your cereal while I eat my toast. Okay?"

"Okay."

"I love you, honey."

"Love you, too. Here's Maris."

After Emma spoke to Maris for a few minutes, she told her she'd call her the following day to give her an update.

Linc was standing at the counter, holding a mug of coffee. During their meal, his gaze had been on her more than it wasn't. She'd eaten because she knew that was best. But she'd kept out of the conversation with Jake and Gillian for the most part. She'd been frustrated with Linc, his attitude and everything that wasn't happening. He knew it. She knew he wasn't the type of man to just let it pass.

She supposed that was a good thing because Barrett had let so many things pass him by. Especially their daughter and watching her grow up as she learned new things about her world and about herself each day. Emma hadn't minded his absence so much for herself. And she supposed now that that fact was telling. But she had minded for Becky's sake.

Emma set her cell phone on the table by the sofa, gearing up for another round with Linc. One way or another, she was going to be kept in the loop.

Trying to keep the tension between them to a minimum, she went to the refrigerator for a bottle of water. Zack had told her to stay away from caffeine. He'd called her with her blood work results before they'd left. Everything had checked out that her tests were normal. She just needed to follow his advice and take better care of herself.

After she plucked a water bottle from the fridge, she unscrewed the lid. She took a few swallows, eyed Linc and asked him, "So are you going to tell me what you and Jake discussed?"

"Not specifically."

She plopped the bottle down on the counter, turned and headed for her bedroom before she said something she'd regret. Or heard something she didn't want to hear.

But Linc had apparently been prepared for her reaction. He stepped in front of her and wouldn't let her pass. "Jake is handling it. He's going to give me a call later, and I might have to go out. That's all you need to know."

He was six feet two of imposing male. Dressed in khakis and an oxford shirt with the sleeves rolled up his forearms, she felt that ever-present pull of attraction even as they went toe to toe. That chemistry between them made her even more frustrated.

"What gives you the right to tell me what I need to know?" she demanded.

"*This* gives me the right."

Before she had time to blink, he'd pulled her into his arms and his lips came down on hers...hard and possessive...as if this kiss would be the answer to everything. Fleetingly she thought of yanking away. But maybe she'd find answers here.

With the feel of his shirt rough against her palms, erotic twinges rushed through her body. That happened whenever she was near Linc. The taste of coffee on his tongue built up all her sensual anticipation. She became fully aware that even though she might not find answers in Linc's arms, she did need an escape from everything that was happening. He was providing her with one.

Before, Linc's kisses had been passionate, but restrained. There was no restraint tonight in his raw hunger. Because they were alone? Or simply because he was tired of holding his desire in check? Tired of letting her freeze him out? Tired of ignoring the obvious chemistry between them?

Everything that had happened between them until now had been heightened by emotions running amuck. How could she figure out what she was feeling for him when her whole world had turned upside down? Right now, Linc wasn't helping that feeling. In fact he was intensifying it a hundredfold. And at this moment, she was letting him.

Suddenly Linc broke off the kiss, put a little space between them and held onto her shoulders. She was aware of his strong muscled forearms. Everything about Linc was strong...including his resolve and his determination to get what he wanted. Yet he possessed an integrity she hadn't experienced with many men.

"If this isn't what you want, I'll go into my bedroom and lock the door. You're safe here with me, Emma. I'm not going to cajole you into something you don't want."

Oh, how she wanted. Those green eyes, that thick dark hair, the slight cleft in his jaw that any woman would want to touch told her a night in his arms could be heaven. Didn't she need heaven right now? Didn't they both?

Feeling a little like Cinderella without a fairy godmother—this man was powerful, rich and full of confidence as he figuratively swept her off her feet—she succumbed to the attraction she'd felt from the first day she'd met him. "Make me forget, Linc. Just make me forget."

With a groan that said he was more than willing, he enfolded her into his arms again, beginning another kiss that could lead them straight to his bedroom. The problem was—they didn't make it to the bedroom.

Their kiss took fire fittingly enough in front of the gas fireplace. His fingers fumbled with her blouse buttons as hers tried to separate the plackets of his shirt. Neither wanted to put a stop to the passion as they kissed. So they grappled with material, popped buttons, and hungrily mated their tongues in kisses that fueled their desire.

Finally his hands were on her bare midriff and hers sifted through his chest hair.

Yes, she wanted to escape. Yes, she wanted to go someplace with Linc she'd never been. How did she know it was possible with him? She just knew. His touch electrified her and made her body tremble in anticipation. Her touch? She couldn't tell exactly how it was affecting him, though he seemed hungry to have her, hungry to rush ahead. Yet hungry to pleasure her, too.

Linc Granger wasn't all about taking his pleasure then falling asleep. He was all about mutual satisfaction.

Her clothes lay strewn across the floor first, but his swiftly followed. Soon they were kneeling before each other on the carpet, fingers in each other's hair, their kisses angling for the finest taste, the most fervent exploration, the deepest kiss. She barely registered her nakedness, the carpet beneath her, the glow from the fireplace. Linc came to her with an urgency she felt, too. They only had this moment in time. Then it would vanish.

She opened her arms to him and wondered what was wrong when he hesitated. But he didn't say a word, just grabbed for his khakis, took a wallet from his pocket and something from there. A condom. He was prepared with a condom. It happened so fast and only took a few seconds. Then he was back, kissing her again, touching her, making her believe she was the only woman in his universe.

When he entered her, she welcomed him. Each thrust pushed her into more glorious sensations...more physical satisfaction than she'd ever known. When she wrapped her legs around his hips, she'd never felt a more perfect union. Her climax shook her body and tumbled her into sensations she'd only ever fantasized about. Linc's release came as she still trembled around him...still held on tight.

With world-shattering intensity she realized she'd fallen in love!

Emma awakened a few hours later, cuddled into Linc's shoulder in his king-sized bed. He'd carried her here, brushed her damp hair from her eyes and then they'd started all over again. They'd touched and satisfied and dozed until she'd forgotten where she was and why she was here. Maybe that had been his purpose. She only knew she'd gotten lost in him.

Something had roused her from sleep and she realized Linc was reaching for his cell phone. He must have put it on the night stand. After kissing her brow, he lifted it to his ear. He listened for a few moments, then said, "I'll be there in fifteen minutes," and clicked off.

Disentangling himself from her, he said, "I have to go out."

"Where?" She realized she was as worried about his safety as much as learning more about her sister.

"We've been through this, Emma. I'll be back as soon as I can. If you need anything, call Gillian. Or the main desk. Ask for the manager. He and I go way back."

"Call Gillian, not Jake? Is he going to be with you?"

When Linc climbed out of bed, Emma couldn't help but admire the good shape he was in— magnificent shape. He was so long-waisted with a flat stomach and slim hips, powerful looking athletic legs. Was he a runner? She didn't even know. Yet she'd slept with him. She'd fallen in love with him.

...And he'd pulled a condom from his pocket as if it was an everyday occurrence.

"What's the matter?" he asked. "Besides the fact I won't tell you what you want to know."

"Nothing."

He sat on the edge of the bed and cupped her chin in his palm. "Liar. I know you, Emma."

"Do you? Do I know you?"

"Where's this coming from? Do you have regrets?"

There was no indication in his voice whether he did or not. And that was part of the problem. What was he feeling?

"I've never had a one-night stand before."

His face still remained neutral though his jaw tightened a little. She wanted to punch his chest and ask—*Didn't the past few hours mean anything to you?*

"What makes you think this was a one-night stand?"

"Wasn't it? You had condoms in your wallet...as if you do this all the time!"

"You would have preferred I didn't protect you? Protect us?"

"That's not my point," she said quietly. "You're the type of man who usually gets what he wants. Tonight you wanted me. I wanted you, too. And I wanted to escape." Her voice cracked on the last word. "But I have a daughter to think of. You have a life that doesn't usually include single moms and their children."

"So much for Google," he said with a shake of his head and a snort of disapproval. "Do you want to know why I don't date a woman more than a few times? And I don't give paparazzi a shot of my personal life if I can help it? I'll tell you. In my last *serious* relationship, the woman I thought I was going to marry had an abortion without telling me."

Emma felt her heart lurch. "Linc—"

"So, yes, I make sure I carry condoms. I'm making sure an accidental pregnancy doesn't ever happen again."

He rose to his feet once more. "I've got to go. Try to get some sleep. I don't know how long this will take."

She hardly had time to catch her breath before he was out the door. A few minutes later she heard the suite door close behind him.

She pulled Linc's pillow to her, cuddled into it, remembering everything about their love-making.

Just where did they go from here?

Following the directions Jake had given him, Linc parked, jogged quickly down a side street and took a right onto an alley. Fifty feet up the alley, he encountered a six foot high fence. His focus wasn't as sharp as it should be. His mind was back in his hotel suite, on the floor in front of the fireplace with Emma...in his bed with Emma...finding sublime satisfaction with Emma. He was truly rattled, not only from having sex with her but from their conversation afterward. He had to get his head on straight and get it on straight now or what he was about to do would be a fiasco.

The fence gave patrons of the Red Door club privacy as they exited the back entrance for a smoke. Somehow Jake had talked his way into the club and kept an eye on Levine who'd been dancing, drinking and smoking weed. They'd learned from his *Branches* page that he was a grad student who liked to party on weekends. Jake had told Linc he wouldn't be able to have a decent conversation with Levine inside the club. The music was too loud, the crowd thick enough for everyone to be bumping into each other. The good news was that Levine seemed to be there alone and hadn't hooked up with anyone. He'd gone out for a smoke before.

Out back, Jake figured Linc could corner Levine even if there were patrons sitting at other picnic tables, drinking and talking. Security was loose. There were bouncers inside the club but not out back. Once Linc had exited his suite, he and Jake had texted for updates and plans.

Now here he was, scaling a fence, hoping like hell the weights and jogging he'd kept up over the years paid off.

Linc landed on the other side of the fence under cover of a palm, balanced on the balls of his feet. In the shadows he made his way around the perimeter until he spotted Levine at one of the tables, a drink in front of him, a cigarette in his hand. Linc didn't know if Jake was outside yet or still inside. He set his phone on vibrate. Whether Jake was covering him or not, now was the time to move.

It was easy to pretend he'd been inside the club. There were a few other picnic tables occupied by groups of twenty-somethings who were either sloshed or stoned because they didn't pay any attention to him or even seemed to notice him. As he crossed to Levine's table and stopped behind him, he spotted Jake exit the back door.

"Mind if I join you?" he asked Levine from behind him.

Levine glanced at Linc over his shoulder, seeming unfazed one way or the other. "I won't be here much longer," Levine said. "It doesn't matter to me."

"Hot date with a missing girl?" Linc asked.

That got Levine's attention. Under the glow of the back door's spotlight, Linc could see the man's pupils were slightly dilated. He'd been more likely than not smoking something other than a Marlboro.

When Levine started to rise, Linc clamped a hand on his shoulder. "I want to talk to you."

Levine glanced toward the back entrance, maybe thinking about calling security. But he saw Jake standing there and must have recognized him. Linc gave Jake a thumps-up sign and Jake returned it.

"Who are you?" Levine croaked.

"It doesn't matter. What matters is that I intend to find out what happened to Paige Trent."

"I don't know anything," the man said desperately, trying to stand again.

But Linc had at least three inches on him, twenty pounds and a hell of a lot of workouts. "I want a play by play. How do you know Paige? And you're not going anywhere until I find out everything you know. My friend and I will make sure of that."

Levine reached into his pocket. But Linc was quicker. He snatched the man's phone. "There's no cause for alarm here unless you have something to hide."

"I'm not hiding anything," Levine muttered weakly.

"Good." He released the guy's shoulder then straddled

the bench beside him. "Then we can have a civil conversation, and both of us can walk away without any broken bones or bruises." Linc had never played this tough guy act before, but now seemed to be the time.

Tim Levine's gaze had dropped to his drink. He appeared to think if he didn't look at Linc or Jake, they'd both go away. That wasn't going to happen.

"Paige's sister Emma is worried sick about her."

"Emma?" Levine asked as if he knew who she was.

Linc considered himself a good judge of character if not a great one. Levine, with his spiked hair and glasses, didn't look as if he'd ever attempted anything criminal or ever could. So Linc decided to appeal to Levine's conscience and see what happened.

"Emma's not eating or sleeping. She passed out the other night. Becky misses Paige, too. So I need to know what you know so she can be found. Emma thinks she's lying in a ditch somewhere or worse yet being tortured by a psychopath. Do you know any psychopaths?"

"I can't say anything," Levine practically moaned. "I promised."

"Promised who?"

When he didn't respond, Linc said, "I'm not going anywhere. Neither is Jake. If we don't pull useful information out of you tonight, we'll keep trying. We might even bring the San Diego police in on it since you obviously know something."

"I got a call from a detective in L.A.," Levine hurried to say. "He asked me all kinds of questions. But I told him I didn't know anything."

"He was probably so busy with homicides, he believed you. But I'm not busy with anything else. I'm on this until I get answers...until Emma gets answers."

Maybe Levine's drunken or pot-induced state wasn't so severe that he blocked out the intensity and purpose in Linc's voice. He seemed to finally understand Linc's determination...because he put his elbows on the table and dropped his head into his hands. "I told Paige this was never going to work. I told her she was making the wrong decisions. I told her hiding out wouldn't solve anything. But she said she didn't know what else to do. She couldn't keep facing Emma—"

A chill ran up Linc's spine—a different kind of chill than he'd experienced thinking about what might have happened to Paige. He didn't have Gillian's skills but he suspected something about this whole scenario was going to hurt Emma deeply.

"Start at the beginning."

Levine took another drag on his cigarette. His hand shook as he laid it on the table, the ember glowing in the dim light.

"You met Paige on *Branches*," Linc prompted.

Levine could obviously hear in Linc's sure tone no reason to deny it. "Yes."

"You were both interested in the same kind of music and the new band Commuter X. Emma knew Paige's password for *Branches*. It was easy to get into her page. Not so easy to go through hundreds of posts to find you. But it wasn't rocket science either."

Linc let the dusky night, the hush broken by revelers at a nearby table, weigh down on Levine.

"I liked Paige," he finally admitted.

"And she liked you."

"Yes, she did," he said with a sigh.

Linc got the distinct impression it wasn't easy for Levine to get dates. Either he was too introverted in everyday life or just lacked social skills. Either way, *Branches* had made it easier to hook up.

"So you took your friendship offline."

"We had some long phone conversations. I was under the impression the cops found my number in her phone records."

"But you told them...?"

"I told them it didn't work out. People meet online. But when they go offline, they usually don't actually connect."

"So then what?"

"Paige confided in me with what was going on with her."

"And just what *was* going on with her?"

Linc almost felt sorry for the guy when he looked positively defeated and started stammering and explaining it all.

When Linc returned to his hotel suite, he found his bedroom empty. No surprise there. Emma had returned to her room. That made a statement.

But he had to speak with her. He had to tell her what he'd discovered. He had a feeling she was going to hate him afterward. He wasn't sure the best way to handle this. Tell her everything he found out? Or lead her to the answers and let fate take its course.

After glancing at Emma's room, Linc went to the wet bar in the living room and checked out the bottles standing there. He poured himself two fingers of the best scotch. He downed it quickly, letting it burn away misgivings and regrets. Confusion remained...and turmoil...and vivid memories of his body joined to Emma's. The unsettling certainty assaulted him that he was perched on the precipice of change, not exactly knowing what that change was going to entail.

Emma's door was slightly ajar. He guessed she'd left it that way so she could confront him when he returned.

With the trip and the stress, the highs and lows of what they'd done must have exhausted her. She was sound asleep. She didn't even stir when he rapped on the door.

The overhead hall light sent some light into the depths of the room...enough that he could see her sleeping on her side, her hands tucked under her chin, her hair sweeping across her pillow. He could just let her sleep until morning, but he guessed she'd resent him for acting as if what he'd learned hadn't meant that much...that *she* hadn't meant that much.

He crossed to the side of the bed where she lay sleeping and switched on the bedside lamp. "Emma?"

His voice must have done it. She came instantly awake. After she levered herself up on her elbow, she punched her pillow behind her. Sitting against the headboard, she practically pulled the sheet up to her chin. She felt as if she had to cover herself now?

His heart sank as he thought about the destruction he was about to rain down on her. On them both. Because what he had to say would forever affect her relationship with her sister.

"I have news." He sat on the edge of the bed and

gazed into her big brown eyes that carried fear and worry in their depths.

"Paige is alive and well," he explained quickly. "She ran away."

Emma shook her head as if to clear it. Her smile was huge as she heard the words that her sister was alive and well. Then the rest of his sentence sunk in. "Why did she run away? Where is she?"

"She's here in San Diego."

The words must have sent adrenaline racing through Emma because she began to scramble off the bed as if she was going to go see Paige right now.

He caught her arm and held her in place. "Wait!"

"I'm not going to wait to see her. Why is she here? Because of Tim Levine? Is she living with him? Why would she hide that from me? Why would she let me think she was...dead?" Emma sounded horrified, though, her intention was still the same—go to Paige as soon as she could.

"Paige has a couple of jobs. Apparently she's using a fake ID that Levine got her on the streets."

Emma mulled that over for an instant. "Has she done something criminal? Robbed a convenience store? What did he get her into?"

"No. Nothing criminal," Linc assured her quickly. "Unless staging her disappearance could be considered criminal. But I doubt it."

"I don't understand why she would stage this whole thing. She wanted me to worry? Oh, Linc. Something's wrong. This isn't Paige. She never wants to cause anyone any hurt or harm."

"That's why she ran away."

"Tell me," Emma demanded, seeing that he'd been leading up to this all along.

"Paige is working two jobs. Levine has a friend with an elderly mother. She needed someone to stay with her mother at night to make sure she doesn't wander off—early Alzheimer's. The family is paying Paige under the table. That's where she is now. I don't think it would be a good idea to barge in there. She's also writing research papers for kids at the college. That's apparently big business. Of course, all of that is under the table, too. That's why there hasn't been a trace of her."

"I still don't understand why she would do this."

Linc could hear the hurt in Emma's voice. Even worse, he knew that was going to magnify monumentally either tonight or tomorrow when she found out the truth.

"I can tell you why she did it. Or you can wait to hear it from Paige. She's renting a studio apartment near the college. It's a sublease so her name isn't on any records. If we're there tomorrow morning when she returns home, she'll stop running when she sees you."

"You can't expect me to wait without knowing everything. Sure, I'd rather hear the reasons from Paige. But I can't wait any longer, Linc. I need to know what she's into and why she ran from me."

There was only one way to say this and that was to say it. "Paige ran away because she slept with your husband. She couldn't face her guilt any longer."

Emma's face drained of all color.

He reached for her. But she eluded his embrace and he knew that was the way it was going to be from now on.

Chapter Seven

"Please leave." Emma's voice shook as she made the request, her heart hurting more than she ever thought possible.

Betrayal battled with astonishment and fought with an overwhelming sense of desolation. What had happened to her life? What had happened to Paige's? What had become of the little sister who had meant everything to her?

She felt as if she were going to fly apart at the seams. Linc had to leave. She couldn't face him feeling like this. She couldn't face him knowing she'd failed as a wife and as a sister. How could any of this have happened?

But he didn't do as she requested. Oh, no. He sat there as still as a stone, staring at her. "Paige is alive," he reminded her.

Yes, Paige was alive. And part of her wanted to jump up and down with joy...or go find her sister and hug her...tell Becky and the world that Paige had been found. Yet this black cloud that came with that news threatened to smother her in sorrow.

Linc shifted closer to her and she wanted nothing more than to hide herself in his arms. But the realization that her husband had betrayed her, had been unfaithful, convinced her to look at Linc differently, too. Her father hadn't known the meaning of vows. He'd left. And now to learn that she herself had chosen wrong...that her husband had tossed their vows as if they were worth nothing...caused her world to totter on its axis.

She needed to know what happened. Her mind was spinning with all the scenarios. But did she really want to know?

"He was older than Paige," Linc said. "He should have been her protector, not at the worst her seducer or at the least succumbed to temptation."

Linc sounded angry and Emma wasn't sure who he was angry with.

"We'll never know what happened." Maybe that was best.

"You don't think you can look into your sister's eyes and see the truth?"

"I don't know if I can look into *anyone's* eyes and see the truth."

Linc looked as if she'd landed a blow. She wanted to say she was sorry. But she was just being honest with him. Earlier she'd given into desire and a passion like she'd never known. But Linc hadn't been able to say what he'd felt. He hadn't been able to say she was important to him...more than an affair that could burn out if another prettier woman came along...or if his schedule got too busy...or he decided she wasn't what he wanted after all.

Barrett had made that decision. He'd turned away and looked to someone else. "Can you leave me alone, Linc? I can't think straight right now. I can't even fathom how I'm going to face her and what I'm going to say. For the past few months, I thought she was dead!"

"You don't want me to help you think this through?"

"You can't. This didn't happen to you. You weren't betrayed by the people you loved most."

"I know what betrayal feels like," he reminded her.

Yes, he did. Someone he'd loved had betrayed him, too.

When Linc stood, he didn't move away immediately. "This man, Tim Levine, really put himself out for Paige. He likes her, and I think she likes him. Apparently this happened during the holidays before Barrett died. I believe Paige confided in Levine because he was a stranger and she didn't have anyone else to turn to."

"She had me! If Barrett forced himself on her, she should have come to me."

"I'm not sure force was involved. I think liquor and bad judgment was. But that's for you to pull out of Paige."

"Why did she run away?"

"Because she didn't want to ruin you memories of Becky's dad. Because your marriage had been sacred to you and she didn't want to spoil that. Because she felt guilty living with you."

"If she felt guilty, then she *did* do something wrong."

"That doesn't mean you can't forgive her. That doesn't mean you can't forgive yourself for not seeing any of this."

"I'll say it again, Linc. This didn't happen to you. I don't even know where to start to begin to deal with it."

"By seeing Paige."

When he bent and stroked her cheek, his thumb dragged against her jawline, reminding her of every place he'd touched...every place he'd kissed.

Finally he did what she'd asked. He left her room.

After he did, her tears began falling and she didn't know if they'd ever stop.

Paige's apartment was located in a stucco building near other stucco buildings of the same ilk. Emma guessed college students were their main renters. She had planned to drive here herself, but Linc had insisted he'd drive her and stay in the car if that's what she wanted.

That wasn't necessarily what she wanted, but that's how it was going to be. She knew Paige might not come home. If Tim Levine had told her that Emma was here, her sister could have chosen to run again. But this time that was her prerogative. This time if she wanted to run, Emma wouldn't stop her. She wouldn't look for her, either. Not again.

Paige's apartment was located to the front of the building, so Emma knew Linc could see her as she propped against the black porch railing. They were going to fly back to L.A. this afternoon...with or without her sister.

When Emma saw Paige hurrying up the street—her job must have been within walking distance—a burst of feeling erupted inside of her including joy and bitterness...relief and pride, embarrassment and disappointment. Her emotions had been in a swirl like this ever since last night. Ever since she'd made love with Linc and decided escape could be forever. But then again, she remembered Linc's withdrawal, the ease with which he'd reached for a condom, the words when he told her that her husband and sister had betrayed her.

Paige stopped when she saw Emma, then slowly approached her. Her sister was only twenty, yet she looked older now. She'd let her short hair grow out, and she no longer sported a blue stripe in the front. She was wearing yellow shorts, a red beaded tank and her ever-present sneakers, carrying an embroidered canvas tote bag with the shoulder strap over her arm.

As she reached the porch, Emma said, "I want to hug you, but I can't. I'm trying to keep an open mind. But I don't know what to say or do."

Tears were running down Paige's cheeks and Emma tried to steel herself against them. But this was Paige, her baby sister. She'd taken care of her when her mother couldn't. She'd taken her in because they were family.

"Will you come inside with me?" Paige asked, searching in her huge tote bag for a tissue, then swiping at her nose.

Emma glanced at the SUV with Linc in it and wished she was there with him...wished even that he was here with her. But how was she going to able to trust again? How was she going to be able to know what to believe?

Instead of waiting for an answer, Paige unlocked

her apartment door, then held the screen. Emma stepped over the threshold, wishing she were anywhere else but here. Inside, Emma noticed a mishmash of furniture, but then Paige's touches here and there—a crocheted shawl over the back of the sofa, colorful woven mats on the end tables, a small sewing machine on a card table with an unfinished project spread across its tray. It looked as if it could be a skirt.

After Emma sat on the sofa, Paige sunk down on the coffee table, facing her. "What are we going to do?" Paige asked the question as if she were six instead of twenty.

"You're going to tell me what happened. All of it."

As Linc had said, when she looked into her sister's eyes, she'd be able to see the truth. What she saw there now was shame, remorse and even self-loathing.

"How long did it go on?" Emma asked, steeling herself for the answer.

"Oh, no! It was nothing like that. Nothing like that," she repeated for emphasis. "I never even thought of Barrett that way. He was like a big brother."

"Some big brother," Emma murmured.

Paige hung her head. "I just don't know how to explain it. You and Barrett were my family. After Mom died, you were everything to me. After you married Barrett, I didn't know how it would be. I didn't know if

I'd be in the way. But we all got along. Barrett didn't seem to care that I was there. In fact, he wasn't even there that much. So it was often like you and me still sharing a place. Then Becky just made everything better. I love playing with her, babysitting her. But then the year before Barrett died, I noticed he...watched me. I had turned eighteen and it was like that changed something between us."

"What did it change?" Emma asked, trying to remember herself, wondering why she hadn't seen whatever was going on.

"You were working more hours. After Maris retired, she began watching Becky instead of you taking her to daycare. When I was home on Thanksgiving break and you'd be working late, I'd put Becky to bed and then Barrett and I would eat together. We joked, we laughed. But there was this...tension in the air. I didn't understand it exactly. I'm not saying I didn't like the attention he gave me. I always liked talking with him from everything about sports to music. But now...there was something else. I wanted to talk to you about it. But how could I? There were no words to explain it. Maybe I was naïve, but I thought Barrett was just missing you."

She took a long breath, studied Emma's face then plunged ahead. "He complained about how Becky had come between you...how after she was born, everything was different. I wasn't completely sure what that meant."

Emma knew exactly what that meant. It meant there were few long candlelit dinners out. It meant Barrett would want lovemaking to continue even if Paige was in the next room or if Becky cried. It meant Emma had Becky on her mind first and her husband's sexual needs second. She'd been at fault here. She just hadn't known the depth of it. Had he resented the fact she'd had care of her sister? He'd married her knowing she did. But then when Becky had come along—

"It happened the Friday after Thanksgiving, your busiest and longest day of the year," Paige said quickly as if she was eager to finally unburden herself. "Barrett came home early with two bottles of wine and a dinner he'd picked up. He'd called earlier and said he didn't want me to worry about cooking. After Becky went to bed, we could warm up the dinner and relax. So that's what we did. He put in a DVD and we ate dinner in the living room. He kept pouring wine and I should have stopped. I shouldn't have had any at all. But he was making me feel so grown-up...so appreciated..." She shrugged and threw up her hands. "I don't know, Em. I just don't know. Before long, my head was swimming. He kissed me. I'd never been kissed like that before!"

With their mom dying, and Paige's introverted nature, she hadn't dated much in high school. Once she'd started college, with all the design projects that she'd had to develop, she hadn't had time for much of a social life. Emma could see the truth in what Paige was telling her. Now she could also see her husband in a different light. She remembered his retreat from meaningful conversation, his late nights, his jealousy of their baby. He'd felt left out and unappreciated. So he'd taken advantage of the one person Emma loved most after Becky...Paige.

Paige's tears were falling again as she recalled everything that had happened. "It all happened so fast! One minute we're laughing at the movie and the next he's kissing me. Then our clothes were almost off and he's whispering to me how this will be our secret. Our secret. I let him do it. I didn't say no."

"Oh, Paige," Emma breathed, crying now too for everything that was lost—her marriage, Paige's innocence, bonds that should have lasted a lifetime. She could see how it had all played out. She could see how Barrett had taken advantage of Paige...how he'd taken revenge for his resentment of the way his marriage had gone. Finally, she could see how Paige had been overwrought with guilt, unsure of what to do, not knowing where to turn.

Without hesitation, Emma leaned forward and wrapped her arms around Paige. They cried together for what they'd both lost...and for the relationship that might never again be the same between them.

Chapter Eight

"Your secretary doesn't look too happy." Jake made this remark as he stepped inside Linc's office without knocking.

"That's because—" Linc tossed down the screenplay he'd been trying to read. "Ah, hell! I snapped at her. I'm going to have to give her an extra vacation day or something." It had been three weeks since he'd returned from San Diego with a silent Emma and a knowing in his gut that she'd backed away permanently.

Jake appeared to not know which subject to tackle first—the extra vacation day or the snapping. "Have you talked to Emma lately?"

Linc glared at him.

But Jake didn't back down. "Have you called her?"

"No, I haven't called her. She's dealing with enough right now."

"How do you know what she'd dealing with if you haven't spoken to her?"

"Don't give me the third degree. Gillian already did that a couple of days ago."

"Answer the question, friend."

Jake's emphasis on the word "friend" made Linc take a figurative step backward. Jake was his friend, a reminder that he could say what was on his mind. So he admitted, "I called Levine. He said Paige was staying in San Diego for the time being. He sounded happy about it. I don't know how Emma feels."

"That's my point exactly. You don't know how she feels. Does *she* know how *you* feel?"

Again Linc kept silent.

Jake's relaxed pose was gone as he lowered himself into the chair in front of Linc's desk with a steady stare. "You're wasting precious time. I recognize the signs. I saw how you looked at Emma. I saw how you responded to her and reacted to her. I saw what you were willing to do to help her. I saw that you cared for her more than you've cared for a woman since I've known you."

"You don't know that," Linc protested just for the sake of doing it, not wanting to admit he cared for Emma more than he'd ever cared for *any* woman.

"I've only known you a few years, that's true. But I've seen your attitude toward women. Do you think I haven't noticed the women you date? I'm a private eye! Emma is different and your feelings toward her seem to be different too. I know what's it's like to fight against something you really want because you don't think you can get it."

Linc knew a little about Jake's marriage to Sara. With a tragedy in his life as a cop, he had planned to never have children. When he and Sara had gotten engaged, she'd agreed to his plan. But then Sara found out she was pregnant and called off their wedding without telling Jake the truth. She hadn't wanted to trap him. Four years later, she told him he had a son.

"I married Sara, thinking I just wanted access to Christopher," Jake continued. "I thought I'd buried everything I'd ever felt for her. But feelings like that don't stay buried. We wasted precious time when we could have been happy. So don't do the same thing, Linc."

"I'm older than she is," Linc muttered.

Jake narrowed his eyes. "Oh, that's a *really* good reason not to be happy."

Unsettling emotions bumping around inside of him, Linc stood and paced. He'd felt like a caged tiger ever since he'd returned from San Diego...ever since he'd said good-bye to Emma, not knowing when or if he'd see her again. He'd vowed he was going to give her time to figure everything out...to accept what had happened and then move forward.

Finally he put his real fear into words. "I'm afraid I took advantage of her and she's never going to be able to forgive that. I shouldn't have started anything let alone—"

He crossed to the window and gazed down at the parking lot, the traffic, the hustle and bustle of his life. His life had meant something different when he was with Emma. Not only with Emma but with her and Becky. Yes, he wanted the opportunity to recapture that. He wanted a chance to—

"How did you leave it with her?" Jake asked practically.

"I...we—" Linc swore again. "She thought she was a one-night stand or that I just wanted an affair."

"And you didn't deny it?" Jake was looking at him as if he was the stupidest man on earth.

"I didn't know what I wanted."

"And now?"

"And now I'm afraid she'll never trust another man...let alone me."

"I can't believe you admitted you're afraid of something. Not the great Linc Granger!"

At another time, Linc might have shot back a sarcastic remark. But right now he knew his arrogance and pride were part of the problem.

"At least let her know you're thinking about her," Jake advised him.

Maybe that would be one step in the right direction. He'd have to find the others on his own.

When the bell over Emma's shop door chimed, she spun toward it, hoping to see Linc. She'd been swallowed by a hurt daze when she'd returned from San Diego. It had taken her a little while to realize that some of that hurt was about Linc. What they'd shared had been spectacular...at least for her. Only afterward, he'd distanced himself. And then she'd distanced herself from him for so many reasons, the main one being trying to sort out all that had happened.

So whenever the phone rang or the door chimed, she hoped it was him. But it never was. Had he just seen himself as her protector and benefactor? Had she misconstrued the rest just as she'd misconstrued her marriage?

Linc didn't walk into her shop now, but Gillian Bradley did. It was near closing time and Emma was glad no one else was in the shop. She'd sent Olivia home early because it had been a slow day.

Gillian crossed to the table where Emma had been arranging new displays. "How are you?"

"Better than I was the last time you saw me."

Gillian's face was full of compassion. "From the vibes I was getting from your sister's jewelry and Tim Levine, I suspected what had happened between Paige and your husband. But Jake and Linc had to confirm it for you. I just wanted to let you know I received your note and your donation for the foundation. How are you and Paige, if you don't mind my asking?"

"We're talking. That's what's important. I still love her so much. And I can forgive what she did."

Gillian appeared to debate with herself for a few moments but then she said, "Paige and Barrett share the blame for what happened. But Barrett was the one at fault. He took advantage of an eighteen-year-old who didn't have enough experience to recognize what was happening." Gillian studied Emma. "But I don't think you need me to tell you that."

Emma shook her head. "No, I don't. I shouldn't have been asleep at the wheel. I should have realized what was going on, especially when Paige didn't come home as often after that Thanksgiving holiday."

"Give yourself a break. After the birth of a baby, a woman's life becomes focused around her child. A supportive husband realizes he can fit into the equation, too. Nathan and I are even closer since Matthew was born. But Nathan is one in a million."

"I guess I wonder if Barrett had other affairs...if I was just convenient at times and he took advantage of that." She gave a wry, humorless laugh. "Yet I guess I wasn't very convenient."

"Does it matter if he had other affairs?"

Now wasn't *that* an interesting question. Did it matter if a man was unfaithful once or a multitude of times? She wasn't sure. "I suppose it doesn't matter."

Gillian stepped away from the new display Emma was arranging to another one. Wooden boxes were filled with masculine gifts. "Actually I came by to do more than catch up with you."

"Do you need a gift basket?" Emma stepped over to the table with her.

"I'm thinking about it." She fingered a mug with the Lakers' emblem and then a classic gold pen. "I have this friend." She stopped. "Well, actually Nathan, Jake and I have this friend. From what we understand, he hasn't been himself lately. He and Nathan went to college together so Nathan knows him really well. He's been growling at almost everyone in his path, and holing up in his house when he's not working."

"Linc?" Emma asked, hoping beyond hope.

"How did you guess?" Gillian's smile was sly.

"We're all pretty sure he misses you."

"He hasn't called," she blurted out.

Gillian's voice took on a more serious note. "I think he might be waiting for you to make the first move. He knows you have a lot to process. Not that I'd interfere in a friend's life," Gillian went on with an innocent look.

That made Emma smile. "Maybe the gift basket should come from *me*."

Emma stood at Linc's front door fortified with the knowledge from Gillian that he was here alone. Emma had never been this nervous. Her knees were practically shaking. She'd wanted to look...good. So she'd bought a new dress, a little more sophisticated than what she usually wore. It was a teal sheath with a short mandarin collar. Keeping her jewelry simple but she hoped elegant, she'd worn dangling gold earrings with her upswept hair, a gold chain bracelet, and white strappy high heels. In her arms she carried a basket with homemade baked goods. What man didn't like baked goods?

If Gillian was wrong and Linc didn't want her in his life, she could simply give him the basket and run. Though running would be tough in these shoes.

The doorbell chime rang through the house. Seconds later, Linc answered the door in denim cut-offs, a black T-shirt and bare feet. Sexy beard stubble lined his jaw and she wondered if he was going for a new look.

At his astonished expression to find her at his door, she became even more nervous. "If this is a bad time or you're busy..."

"No, not busy. I just came in after a walk on the beach. I took a few days off this week. I was just—" He gave her a smile that didn't reach his eyes, then finished with, "I was just relaxing."

Linc relaxing. That was a novel thought. An awkward silence fell between them.

"I brought you a...a...thank-you gift." She held out the basket to him.

"No thanks necessary." He studied the basket as if her gratitude wasn't a good thing, but then stepped back. "Would you like to come in?"

"Sure," she responded, relieved.

He took the basket from her and led her into his living room. She hadn't been inside his home before. It was beautiful with its teak floor and sea and earth colors everywhere. There was a magnificent ocean view through the large picture window. The house was unassuming but quality through and through. A large ceiling fan spun between the exposed rafters of the cathedral ceiling.

He set the basket on the coffee table, then turned to her as if he had something on his mind.

Before he could start, though, she plunged in. "I'm sorry, Linc."

His face remained expressionless. "Sorry about what?"

"For shutting you out. After you told me about Paige and Barrett, I closed down and I pushed you away. If you don't want to see me again, I understand. It's not as if we've known each other very long. And I come with a lot of baggage, not to mention a little girl—"

He cut her off by reaching for her and enfolding her into his arms, those strong arms she loved so much.

"You don't have anything to apologize for. I never should have taken advantage of you like I did."

"Taken advantage?"

"Yeah. That night in my suite I should have stayed the hell away from you. You were too vulnerable. I knew that. But I just pushed what you needed aside."

"That's not true," she protested with feeling. "You *gave* me what I needed. I needed you that night, Linc. And I'm going to tell you something that might make you want to push me back out the door. I'd realized that night that I'd fallen in love with you."

Stark silence. Then he asked in a gravelly voice, "In love with me?"

She started to pull away, not exactly sure what he was feeling, believing her declaration was a total surprise and not something he wanted to hear.

But he caught her, pulled her closer against him and said, "Don't you go anywhere. Neither of us is going to run from this. Not any more. Ever since we got back, I've been stewing about what I should have done and shouldn't have done. Jake finally made me realize why. I love you, Emma Henderson. I know you've been through a lot. And I'll give you all the time you need. Becky needs to get to know me. But I won't have this silence between us again. In fact, it was going to stop tomorrow."

He gave her a crooked grin. "I called Maris and made her an accomplice. Tomorrow while you were at work, she was supposed to let the florist in. Since your favorite color is pink—she told me it was—you were going to have pink roses from one end of your house to the other. This afternoon I was just walking the beach, wondering if I was making a mistake, wondering if I should give you more time—"

She wrapped her arms around his neck. Lacing her fingers in his hair, she nudged his head toward hers. "Are you going to kiss me?"

"Always," he murmured, a moment before his lips covered hers.

It was a kiss with enough passion to last a lifetime.

Epilogue

The evening candlelight service in the small church Emma attended began with a harpist playing delicate, joyful music. In her cream satin gown with a wreath of pink sweetheart roses woven into her hair, Emma took Becky's hand and started down the white runner. Standing at the end of the aisle, tall, broadshouldered and smiling, in a tuxedo that made him seem even larger than life, Linc waited for her.

The past six months had been a journey of discovery for them both. In San Diego, she'd wondered about her ability to trust a man again. But Linc made trusting easy...just as he had from the very beginning. He was a man whose actions spoke louder than any words. He was a protector and a defender, and she often had to stand up for what she wanted to do. She had to stand her ground to keep her independence. The terrific thing about that was he seemed to like that quality in her!

She was also learning to compromise and found the happiness that came from doing that with Linc was more important than independence. Loving Linc meant letting him take the lead sometimes, letting him provide for her and Becky what she never could. On his part, and with kind understanding, Linc was letting her work out her relationship with Paige.

They'd decided to get married this week before Christmas so they could celebrate Christmas together at Linc's house as a family. Paige was going to stay throughout the holidays, and Emma was hoping they'd find again the bonds they'd once shared.

Standing in the first pew, Paige took Becky's hand and smiled at her sister with the hope that she could put things right. As Emma glanced around at Jake, his wife Sara, their son Christopher, at Gillian and Nathan and their little boy Matthew, at Maris and Olivia and Earl, she felt the full promise of the life she was going to share with Linc.

Linc took her hand as she stepped up to the altar to stand with him before the minister. Linc leaned close and whispered, "I love you."

Happy tears filled her eyes as she whispered back, "I love you, too."

After the minister spoke a few words of welcome, he said, "I understand you've written vows for each other."

Linc and Emma faced each other, their hands joined.

At the minister's nod, Emma went first. "I, Emma Henderson, take you, Lincoln Granger, to be my husband, best friend, and life partner. I promise to honor, love and respect you. I will try to fill each of your days with happiness, unwavering loyalty, and my desire to be the best wife to you I can possibly be. Becky already loves you. I vow to always consider your wishes when raising her, to let you be the dad you want to be. I love you, Linc, and I will love you and be devoted to you beyond my last breath."

She could see her promises had touched him. He gave her a crooked smile and cleared his throat. Then in a husky voice, he began, "Emma Henderson, you've changed my world. I'd always dreamed of having a family, but felt that dream was just out of my reach. Until I met you. You put the sparkle in my day and..." He leaned close to her and murmured in her ear, "The passion in my nights." Then he straightened again and squeezed her hand. "You and Becky are the gifts I never expected to receive. And this Christmas will be the most joyous one I've ever experienced. I promise you that you will never doubt how devoted I am to you...how much I love you. I vow to honor, respect and cherish you every single day. Always."

Emma's throat tightened again, hearing the word that was so important to her...and so important to Linc. They'd had it engraved in their wedding bands— *Always*.

Moments later, he slipped her wedding band on her finger and she slid an identical band on his. They had no doubts about the strength and power of their love.

After the minister gave his final blessing, he smiled at them broadly. "You may kiss and seal your vows."

They did.

Always wouldn't last nearly long enough.

From the Author

ALWAYS DEVOTED is Book 3 in my Search For Love series. It is a never-before-published novella. In the first book of the series, Nathan's Vow, I introduce Linc Granger as Nathan's best friend. He was definitely hero material and I had to write a story just for him! Though my forte is usually romance, I decided to go a little more mainstream with this one and add some mystery for a change of pace. I think you'll fall in love with Linc and feel deeply for Emma and her daughter. But I also believe you'll want to find the answer to—What happened to Emma's sister?

Throughout all my books (over 80 now), I attempt to keep the emotion of my characters as the focus. My intention is always to touch my readers' hearts and urge them to believe in happily-ever-after. Living in Pennsylvania with my college sweetheart and three cats, I spend most days writing, editing, cooking and gardening. I draw inspiration from music, the farm in my back yard, and my hummingbird garden. Relationships have always fascinated me and I look forward to writing about them for a long time to come. For more about me and my latest releases, including excerpts, photos and short stories, please visit my website at www.karenrosesmith.com. To keep in touch day to day, follow me at Facebook and on Twitter!

KAREN ROSE SMITH BOOKS
AVAILABLE IN E-BOOK FORMAT

SEARCH FOR LOVE Series
*Nathan's Vow, Book 1 **

*Jake's Bride, Book 2 **

*Always Devoted, Book 3 **

*Always Her Cowboy, Book 4 **

Heartfire, Book 5

*Cassidy's Cowboy, Book 6 **

*Her Sister, Book 7 **

FOREVER LOVE Series
*April's Promise **

FINDING MR. RIGHT Series
*Kit and Kisses, Book 1 **

Forever After, Book 2

*When Mom Meets Dad, Book 3 **

*Falling For Her Boss, Book 4 **

*Toys and Baby Wishes, Book 5 **

Love in Bloom, Book 6

*Ribbons and Rainbows, Book 7 **

*Wish on the Moon, Book 8 **

*A Man Worth Loving, Book 9 **

EVERYDAY LOVE Short Story Series
Everyday Cinderellas, Vol. 1
Everyday Prince Charming, Vol. 2
Everyday Romance, Vol.3

Garden of Fantasy
Abigail and Mistletoe
Writing is a Business

SCIENCE FICTION
SHORT STORY COLLECTION
Journey Into Chaos

BOXED SETS
Finding Mr. Right Box Set One
Finding Mr. Right Boxed Set Two
Search For Love Boxed Set One
Search For Love Boxed Set Two
Everyday Love Boxed Set

* Also available in audio book format

Excerpt from HER SISTER
Search For Love series, Book 7

Prologue

*W**here is Lynnie? Where did she go?*

In her mind, five-year-old Clare Thaddeus called to her little sister—*Come back, Lynnie. Please come back.*

The huge policeman crouched down in front of Clare's mother at the sofa and said in a deep, slow voice, "Mrs. Thaddeus, I know you're terribly upset. But I need details. We've got an hour before daylight. If your daughter wandered outside—"

Clare's father, who'd been talking to another man in blue, glanced at her, and Clare huddled down deeper into the big green armchair. Her dad didn't come to her but rather went to her mom, sank down beside her and wrapped his arm around her. Then he spoke to the officer. "Our daughter, Lynnie, is three. She would never go outside into the dark on her own."

"Tell us again where you were last night," the policeman demanded in a not-so-nice voice.

"I worked late, preparing a brief."

"Until five a.m.?"

"Yes, until five a.m. As I told you, I always check the girls' rooms before turning in. Lynnie wasn't in her bed. I woke my wife. We looked through the whole house and then we called you."

Clare had been sleeping in her brand new room. They'd moved in here—she studied her hand and counted her fingers—five days ago. Boxes were still stacked down here and upstairs. The house was okay. There were more rooms for her and Lynnie to play hide and seek. But she didn't like being alone in her own room at night. She'd liked it better when she and Lynnie had slept in the same room.

Earlier she'd thought she'd heard Lynnie's door open...thought her sister was going to the bathroom and might come in and crawl into bed with her. But she'd been *so* sleepy. She and Lynnie had been running through the hose sprayer all afternoon in the backyard while Mommy unpacked. She was supposed to watch her sister. She was always supposed to look out for Lynnie. That's what big sisters did.

Where had Lynnie gone?

Then Clare remembered the blue car that had driven

down the alley in back of the yard lots of times. The man had stopped once and watched them. But she'd thought he might be one of their new neighbors who just wanted to say hi.

Should she tell the policeman?

He was so big, and he looked mad. Her dad looked mad, too, as he asked, "Why do you want to question me and my wife separately?"

"That's just the way we do it, Mr. Thaddeus."

Although she was scared of the two big men in blue uniforms, she knew her mommy and daddy wouldn't let them hurt her. Policemen helped, didn't they? They were going to help find Lynnie.

She slipped off of the chair, went over to the sofa and tugged on her mother's arm. "Mommy, when I was playing—"

The doorbell rang.

"Are you expecting someone?" the policeman asked, his brows arched.

Not sounding at all like herself, her mother answered, "I called a friend."

"Before or after you called us?"

Her mother's face turned red. "*After*, of course."

"Mommy." She tugged on her mother's arm again while one of the policemen went to the door.

Her mother took Clare's hand. "Not now, honey.

Natalie's going to take care of you for a little while so we can talk to the officers."

"But, Mommy—"

Her mom's best friend, Natalie Barlow, rushed into the living room looking as upset as her mom and dad. "What can I do?"

Her father answered quickly. "Can you take Clare upstairs? And can you call our old neighbors? Maybe they'll help search. I've got to get out there looking, but I have to finish answering questions first."

Natalie gave Clare a weak smile and took her hand. "Come on, honey. Let's go upstairs for a while."

Her mom kissed her.

Her dad gave her a nod.

She tried again. "When I was playing with Lynnie—"

Tears fell down her mom's cheeks. Her dad said, "Not now. Go upstairs with Natalie."

What she had to say wasn't important. The man in the blue car didn't matter. Only Lynnie mattered.

As Clare followed Natalie upstairs, she got very afraid. What if the policemen couldn't find Lynnie? Is that why her mommy was crying? Because she didn't think they could? Was that why her dad was mad?

Natalie bent down to her. "I don't want you to worry. Everything's going to be all right."

But Clare knew better. If Lynnie didn't come home, nothing would ever be right again.

Chapter One

"I'm not taking it back. I bought it with my own money." Shara Thaddeus stared at her mother defiantly, standing her ground. At sixteen, she was Clare's payback for the trouble Clare had given her parents when she was sixteen, though certainly not for the same reason.

At thirty-two and a single parent, Clare didn't know what to do with Shara any more than her parents had known what to do with her. She'd rebelled because she'd wanted their attention. *Any* of their attention. All of their attention. When Lynnie had been around, Clare had loved her and protected her and been her big sister. But after she'd disappeared, it was as if Clare hadn't existed. Everything was always about Lynnie. And Clare had just wanted her parents to realize that although her sister was gone, *she* was still there.

Shara, on the other hand, had always had all of Clare's attention. What she didn't have was a father. She'd been a precocious child, constantly testing her boundaries. Sometimes Clare just got weary of being a watchdog. But yet wasn't that what parents were supposed to do?

After taking a deep breath for patience then putting her chin-length brown hair behind her ears, she reached out and took the blouse from Shara's hands. It really wasn't a blouse, just a stretch lace concoction that *her* daughter wasn't going to be caught dead in. "If you wear this out on the street, you'll get arrested. What did you buy to go with it?" She meant to keep her tone curious but it sounded judgmental anyway.

Shara produced a pair of black leather shorts that Clare suspected would fit too snugly.

"The outfit goes back. It's not appropriate for school. It's not appropriate to wear to the mall. It's not appropriate to be caught dusting the house in. What were you thinking?"

"I'm thinking there are a few boys who would think I'm hot."

Counting to ten had never been a strategy that worked well for Clare, especially when her daughter was deliberately trying to push her buttons. But she tried it again, nonetheless, not meeting with any more success than she'd achieved the last time. She prayed for patience, or wisdom or anything that would help deal with her daughter.

Finally, in a friendly tone she asked, "Care to give me their names? Maybe I can do background checks."

Shara studied her mother, trying to decide if she was joking or serious. "Brad said he likes me in black."

"Brad doesn't need to like you in anything. He's a senior. You're a sophomore. We've talked about this, Shara. He has a reputation and I don't want him giving *you* a reputation."

"You are wound *so* tight," Shara mumbled.

Before Clare could deal with *that* assessment, the telephone rang. She glanced at it, thought about letting it ring, letting the answering machine take over. But maybe both she and her daughter needed a few minutes to cool down. She saw from the Caller ID that it was her mom's home number. This would probably be a short conversation. They never had much to say to each other.

Clare watched Shara take the new outfit and her other bags to her room. "They go back," Clare called after her.

Her daughter didn't bother to reply.

Clare greeted her mom with a chipper "hello,"

wondering what she was going to put together for supper. As an X-ray technician at the hospital, she usually arrived home after Shara. Today, however, Shara had asked her if she could stop at the mall for an hour or so after school and Clare had agreed. It looked as if they'd both be taking a trip after supper to return Shara's purchases. Maybe they should just leave now and grab pizza there. The mall on an October Friday night would be busy.

"Clare?"

The tiny crack in her mother's voice made Clare pull in a breath. "What's wrong? Has something happened to Dad?"

Although her father and mother had divorced two years after Lynnie had disappeared, Clare had desperately tried to hold onto bonds with both of them.

"I haven't heard from your father in weeks. The last time I saw him was at the picnic you had Labor Day weekend."

It was really strange. Her parents had once had a good marriage until Lynnie was taken. Now they were awkward together whenever they had to be in the same room. Clare always felt as if she were the cause of that awkwardness, always felt as if she should do something to make it all better, always felt as if she was the neutral territory in the middle of a decades-old war.

After a short pause, her mother explained, "Detective Grove called me. He already spoke to your father."

Clare's heart skipped a beat. "Detective Grove?" The picture of a tall lean man in a rumpled suit flashed in her mind—the man who had taken over Lynnie's investigation after the patrol officers' first visit.

"Do you remember him?" her mother asked gently—too gently—and Clare had a shivery premonition of what could be coming.

"Didn't he retire?" she asked her mom, her heart racing now.

"Yes, he did. But he's not really keen on retirement and he's been...working a few cold cases." Her mother's voice was edgier than usual and a little wobbly, too.

"What are you trying to tell me, Mom?" Clare's hands became sweaty as she thought about all the possibilities. Lynnie's face at three and a half was still so vivid in her mind—the face they'd used on posters...the face she'd envisioned floating in a river...the face on the body in nightmares that had been buried in a ditch. The *not* knowing had always been worse than knowing. The not knowing is what had torn them all apart. Clare really believed that if the police had found Lynnie's body somewhere, maybe they could have gone on as a family.

Maybe.

"He wants to meet with us tomorrow morning. You, me and your dad. He thinks he has a lead."

Clare's throat went desert dry. Even though she'd only been five, she remembered the hope that had filled her parents' faces whenever a new lead had been phoned in, whenever the police had gotten a tip from an informer on the street, whenever there was a chance that Lynnie might have been spotted. She also remembered the expression on their faces when all those hopes had been dashed and one day had turned into the next without teaching them anything new.

Except that they were losing each other, hour by hour, day by day, week by week.

"What kind of lead?" Clare asked, trying to control the shakiness in her voice.

"He wouldn't tell me over the phone. He's working out of his home, so I offered the use of my office at *Yesteryear*. Can you be there tomorrow at ten?"

Her father wouldn't like meeting at her mother's shop. Now and then he'd complained to Clare that her mother was lost in the past. He didn't like the mustiness of the store or what the old furniture represented—a history that couldn't be changed...a child who would never come home. Her mother didn't see it that way at all. Her mother liked to relive every memory she had. She wrapped herself in the reminiscence of what she told Clare were the happiest years of her life. More than that, *Yesteryear* had given her a reason to get up each day, a reason to search for old furniture if not for her daughter, though Clare suspected she still looked for Lynnie everywhere she went.

Trying to prepare herself for the meeting, she shored up her courage and asked, "Did Detective Grove say whether this lead means Lynnie's alive or dead?"

A sharp intake of breath met her question and then her mom answered, "He didn't say, and I didn't ask. I still have hope, Clare. I always have."

Yes, her mother had held onto the hope that Lynnie was still alive, that some misguided woman had taken her and raised her for her own. But a misguided woman didn't steal a child from someone's house in the middle of the night.

False hope was worse than no hope at all. Clare and her dad understood each other on that one point, at least.

"I'll be there tomorrow, Mom, but please don't—" She wasn't sure how to say it.

"Please don't believe in the best rather than the worst? Oh, Clare. Maybe as you get older you'll learn that believing in the best is the only way to get through some days. I'll see you in the morning, honey."

Clare and her mother weren't on the same wavelength...would never be on the same wavelength. Just like her and Shara?

She said goodbye, hung up the phone and went to her daughter's room. Arguing with Shara would postpone thinking about the meeting tomorrow morning...a meeting that could shake up all of their lives once more.